Murder and Mistletoe

Samantha Baca

Silver Falls Duet

Snowed Inn For Christmas
Murder and Mistletoe

Content Warning

Violence/ Domestic Violence

Murder

Stalking

Explicit language and sexual content

Contents

One	1
Two	3
Three	7
Four	15
Five	19
Six	23
Seven	31
Eight	37
Nine	41
Ten	47
Eleven	53
Twelve	59
Thirteen	63
Fourteen	65
Fifteen	73
Sixteen	83
Seventeen	89
Eighteen	93
Nineteen	95
Twenty	99
Twenty One	109
Twenty Two	113
Twenty Three	119
Twenty Four	127
Twenty Five	131
Twenty Six	137
Twenty Seven	141
Twenty Eight	151
Twenty Nine	155
Thirty	163

Thirty One	167
Thirty Two	171
Thirty Three	173
Thirty Four	181
Thirty Five	185
Thirty Six	189
Thirty Seven	191
Thirty Eight	197
Thirty Nine	203
Forty	207
Forty One	213
Other Books By Samantha Baca	219
Acknowledgments	223
About the Author	225

One
Poppy

I grunted as I slammed the shovel into the ground, trying to break through the dirt as a bead of sweat dotted my brow. I looked around to make sure the woods were still as quiet as they were when I dragged the body out here a while ago. It was supposed to be quick and easy—dig a hole big enough to dump his wretched body into, visit my cousin so I had an alibi for being in Silver Falls, and then get the hell out of town. I somehow didn't account for the ground being frozen with a nice layer of snow and ice covering most of it, or how fatigued my body would be after dragging his lifeless body out of the house and shoving him into the car. I was relying on caffeine and adrenaline to keep me going.

I took a deep breath and lifted the shovel again, stopping when I heard the unmistakable sound of footsteps. Panic seized me as my eyes darted around the forest, trying to pinpoint the direction they were coming from. I didn't have time to run without being caught, and I sure as hell didn't have the luxury of just abandoning the body and pretending I was never there. My footsteps alone would be a good indication that someone was here and that the asshole didn't just come out into the middle of the woods to die the brutal death he had been dealt.

My hands trembled as I tried to focus enough to figure out what to do. The footsteps got louder, and I looked up just in time to lock eyes with the one person I never thought I would see again.

"Poppy?" Patrick asked, stopping a good foot away from me as he took the earbud out of his ear and looked at me. "What are you doing out—"

His words stopped abruptly as he looked from me to the shovel in my hand to the dead body on the ground in front of me.

Fuck.

Two
Patrick

I stepped closer, getting a better look at the man who was hardly recognizable due to the bruising on his face. I lifted my eyes and looked at Poppy, since she was my main concern at the moment.

"What the fuck is going on?" I asked, staring at her as she squirmed beneath my gaze.

"It's not what it looks like," she said, her cheeks flushing red with heat despite the cold air around us.

"Really? Because it looks like you're standing over a dead body and trying to dig up frozen dirt to bury it."

"Okay," she replied softly as she rocked back on her heels. "It's exactly what it looks like."

I shook my head, trying to clear the fog that threatened to take over. I hadn't seen Poppy in at least ten years, maybe longer. She was never close with her family and didn't come around often. I had met her a few times when Gage's family had their reunion at the inn, but she always stayed to herself and was quick to leave as soon as she could.

"Does Gage know you're in town?" I asked, folding my arms over my chest.

She shook her head and looked away.

"Were you planning on telling him?"

"Yeah. I was going to go by and visit before I left."

She looked away from me, and I could tell she was hiding something.

"I'm guessing you didn't come to town just to see him and say hi."

"Nope."

I nodded as all of the pieces started to fall into place.

"What's the deal with the dead guy?"

"He's my husband."

My eyebrows rose involuntarily at the news that she had gotten married. While Poppy didn't keep in touch with her family, I was still surprised no one had mentioned her marriage. Perhaps they didn't know…

"It was a shotgun wedding in Vegas. We were drunk and stupid. He wanted me to be his *free use* toy. I wanted a divorce. It was our many differences in opinions that led us here." She extended her hands in front of her while holding the shovel under her arm.

"You killed him because he wouldn't give you a divorce?"

"No." Her features sobered as she stared down at him with nothing but rage and fury in her eyes. "I killed him because he was going to kill me."

I noticed the bruises along her neck and the faint bruise on her cheek, which she had tried to cover with makeup. My blood boiled as I continued to stare, taking note of every possible injury on her.

"He tried to kill you." It wasn't a question, just a fact that tasted sour on the tip of my tongue as I said it out loud.

"Several times. We got married six months ago, and my life has been a living hell ever since. I tried to leave so many times, and every time the punishment got worse. A few months ago, I ended up in the ICU because of how badly he hurt me."

"Fuck, Poppy. Did you go to the police and tell them what he did?"

"How could I when he was the sheriff of the small town we lived in? No one would have believed me, Pat. I did what I had to do, and I don't regret it. He won't hurt another woman ever again, so I can live with what I did."

I pressed my lips together and exhaled heavily through my nose. I looked around, making sure we were still by ourselves. There weren't any cabins nearby, which I loved because it was always calm and quiet on my morning runs, unlike what I used to experience when I lived in New York. Minus today, when my morning run was interrupted by finding my best friend's cousin trying to bury her dead husband.

"Give me the shovel," I said, stepping closer and extending my hand to take it.

"What?" she asked, her eyes widening in disbelief.

"The shovel, Poppy. Hand it to me. We don't have much time."

"Pat, you don't have to do this. I don't want to get you caught up in my mess."

"It's a little too late for that. The quicker we can get him in the ground, the better."

She handed me the shovel, and I ignored the spark of electricity that ran through me as our gazes locked again. I'd always been attracted to Poppy, not that I would ever do anything about it. Hell, even if I wanted to, Gage had always made it clear that she was off limits—much like my younger sister, whom he was now dating. But now wasn't the time to worry about any of that as the sun continued to rise, casting a warm glow in the sky above us.

I took a deep breath and let it out, hoping this wouldn't be something I would later regret.

Three
Poppy

"Get in the truck," Patrick said as he tossed the shovel into the bed.

"That's not necessary. I can walk back to the inn."

After Patrick found out that I had driven Dale's car, he suggested that we put Dale back in the driver's seat and push the car into the river to make it look like he lost control and died that way. I knew that if they did an autopsy, it would show blunt force trauma to the head instead, but I didn't have time to worry about all of that. Hopefully, it would be days, if not weeks, before the car surfaced and anyone found his body.

He had been a good sport and didn't complain about the physical work, while I struggled not to compliment him on his killer body when he took his hoodie off and tossed it to the side when he got too hot. We were there for a reason, and that reason did not include checking out my cousin's best friend.

"The last thing you need is your footprints leading from the grave to the inn. Get in the truck, and I'll drive you into town. We'll make it look like I picked you up from the airport or something."

"Why would you do that?"

"Because you need an alibi. It's already daylight, so you can't sneak around without someone noticing you and asking questions. Has anyone in town seen you yet?"

"No," I answered quickly with a shake of my head. "I got in super early this morning and came directly here."

"Well, at least we don't have to worry about the car," he said as he looked off in the distance, where we had pushed it into the river. "Good thinking with wearing gloves and not touching anything. Even if it's his car, you don't want your fingerprints to be the ones they pull first."

"Thanks. I guess old habits die hard," I replied softly, feeling his eyes as he studied me. It wasn't a surprise that I spent a lot of my teen years and early twenties getting into trouble. It was one of the reasons my family didn't want me around. I brought more trouble than it was worth, and they got tired of cleaning up my messes. *If they could only see me now and the mess I had gotten myself into.*

"You're not the same reckless teenager with a bad attitude that you used to be," he said sternly, giving me a look.

"Really? Cause this doesn't seem like something a mature, responsible adult would get themselves into." I pointed out the window to where the car was, hopefully sinking in the river.

"Don't do that."

"Do what?" I lifted my hands in front of me. "Speak the truth? I fucked up, Pat. Big time. Anyone can see that, and now you're caught up in the mess I created."

"I'm not caught up in anything, Poppy. You didn't fuck up—your husband did the second he laid his hands on you. He deserved what happened to him."

"How can you say that so easily?" I asked as I stared at him, wondering what had made him so cold and calloused.

"Any man who puts his hands on a woman doesn't deserve to take another fucking breath. Do I make myself clear on where I stand on this?" He pinned me with a look that sent a shiver down my spine.

I nodded and looked out the window as he put the truck in drive and started going slowly in circles.

"What are you doing?"

"Erasing our footsteps and making it less obvious that any dirt was dug up. This will look like someone went off-roading and got turned around. If we're lucky, the car will float far away from here, so no one will bother looking in this area to begin with. But I'd rather not leave that to chance and don't want anyone to question the fresh shovel marks."

"Do you think that will work?"

"It's the best option we have right now."

I let out a long, slow exhale and leaned against the seat, noticing how everything around me smelled like him.

****

Thirty minutes later, Patrick was pulling into the diner on Main Street and helping me out of the truck.

"I know you want to put on a show and give me an alibi, but you don't have to do all of this," I whispered through clenched teeth as his hands wrapped around my waist while he helped me out of the truck. My whole body trembled as my teeth chattered, but the warmth of his hands on me sent heat straight through me.

"I'm not putting on a show. I'm taking you to breakfast."

"But you don't *have* to. I can seriously walk to the inn, say hi to Gage, and get the hell out of here." I forced a smile at an older woman as she walked past us on the sidewalk while we stood by his truck.

A gust of cold air whipped past us, making me shiver harder than before. When I packed Dale into the car and left last night, it was unexpected. There hadn't been time to grab anything that I might have needed—like a winter jacket. I had a hoodie and leggings on, which was practically the same as wearing a bikini, given how warm they kept me. I remembered it being cold in Silver Falls this time of year, but never *this* cold.

"When was the last time you ate?" he asked, standing in front of me with his legs spread and arms folded over his chest as he waited for the answer, blocking me in so I couldn't get past him.

I closed my eyes, trying to force the memories of last night out of my brain.

"You don't say no to me," Dale snarled, slapping me across the face, the pain of it leaving an immediate sting. "You will do as I say, when I say it."

"No." I jutted my chin out and stared him down, making

sure he knew I had enough. We had just finished dinner, and I was still cleaning up when he came in and demanded sex.

"No? No? I'll teach you some fucking manners." He raised his fist and slammed it toward my face, but I jumped out of the way, forcing him to lose his balance and stumble into the wall. The smell of whiskey permeated the air as he growled and cursed me under his breath as he stared at his hand that had scraped the wall.

I knew that I had to act now or I wouldn't have a chance later. I grabbed the frying pan from the counter that I hadn't put away and clenched the handle tightly in my fist. As soon as he turned to face me, I swung full force, a sickening thud as the pan collided with his cheekbone.

His face turned red as he held a hand to the spot that I hit.

"You stupid bitch. You're going to pay for that."

I swung again, knowing that I had to make it count.

But he was stronger and faster than I was, stopping the pan before it could hit him. He pulled the pan out of my grip and tossed it to the floor before storming toward me with fire raging in his eyes. His hand shot out, grabbing my throat as he slammed me against the wall, pinning me in place with his body.

I felt a rush of air escape as I tried to stay conscious. His grip on my throat got tighter as I clawed at his skin to try to get free. I was able to move just slightly, giving me the opportunity to hit him where it counted.

I brought my knee up hard and fast, watching as his face morphed into pain as he let go of me and bent over. There was no doubt in my mind that he would kill me tonight.

He'd already made that clear.

While he was bent over, I grabbed the cast-iron pan from the stove and whacked him on the back of the head. His body fell forward from the impact, but I didn't trust that it was a fatal blow. I rolled him over and hit him again, this time aiming for the side of the head. Once I was sure he was knocked out, I pressed the pan down hard against his throat with all of the strength I had until a few minutes had passed.

I stepped back and stared at his lifeless body on the floor as nausea washed over me.

I just killed my husband.

"Poppy?" Patrick asked, his brows furrowed as he stared at me.

"I'm sorry, I totally missed that. What did you say?"

"I asked when the last time you ate was. But given that you're suddenly as pale as a ghost, I'm going to say you need to eat." He nodded toward the diner and stepped onto the sidewalk, waiting for me to follow. "I'm not asking, Poppy."

I tilted my head to the side and studied his features as I stood in front of him. He was taller than I remembered as I lifted my hand to shield my eyes from the sun as I stared up at him.

"You're not the boss of me," I said, pulling my shoulders back. "You can't just demand that I go inside and eat."

He chuckled and worked his jaw back and forth before moving so quickly that I didn't have time to process what was happening until I was pressed against his truck while his body towered over mine. He leaned down and pushed my hair out of the way as he whispered in my ear.

"I may not be the boss of you, but as long as you refuse to take care of yourself, I will step in and make sure it gets done. Do I make myself clear?"

His breath was hot against my neck, sending tingles across my skin and creating a slight ache between my thighs.
I knew Patrick would never cross any boundaries that I set, but I couldn't help but feel a thrill at how turned on I was by his commanding attitude. It was also so incredibly strange how different it felt to have him in my space compared to how it felt when Dale would get too close. I hadn't seen Patrick in years, yet I felt safer with him than I had ever felt with anyone.

I sucked in a breath and held it as I made the stupid mistake of looking up and into his emerald green eyes.
"Now, Poppy." He licked his lips, his eyes locked on mine, never wavering as he extended his hand and pulled me off the truck.

My legs felt wobbly as I made my way into the diner, ignoring the heat that continued to blossom inside the longer his hand stayed planted on my lower back.

14

<u>Four</u>
Patrick

We sat in a booth toward the back of the diner with me facing the entrance so I could keep an eye on anyone coming in or out. While Poppy had spent a lot of time in Silver Falls growing up, it had been years since she'd been back, and I didn't want her to feel overwhelmed if anyone came up to talk to her. At least I could use my grumpy exterior to ward off most people. I wanted her to see Gage and decide whether she was staying in Silver Falls before I let the nosy bodies of Silver Falls get close to her.

It was busy at the diner, so it took our waitress a few minutes to get to us. She hurried over, grabbing the pencil from behind her ear as she whipped out her notepad and stood at the end of the table.

"I'm so sorry about the wait. We're a little busier than normal with the holidays," she said, offering me a smile before looking at Poppy. "Hi! I don't think we've met. I'm Terry."

She extended her hand to Poppy, who took it nervously and attempted to smile back at her.

"Poppy."

"Nice to meet you. I swear, I don't think I've seen Pat with anyone besides Gage and Julie. I've been wondering when he'd stop being so grumpy and make some friends," Terry teased, nudging me with her elbow before rubbing a hand along her very pregnant, very swollen stomach. Terry was happily married and had been trying to play the town matchmaker since the day she found out I was single when I first came in, almost a year ago, when I first moved there.

"I have to be grumpy, it keeps people away from me," I teased back, as I leaned against the plush fabric of the booth.

"Well, apparently it didn't work for Poppy. At least she doesn't seem to think you're too grumpy."

"He hasn't been grumpy with me, but maybe he just likes me more than the others," Poppy said, grinning at me. She was up to something. I could tell by the devious smile playing at the corners of her lips.

"Does that mean you two…." Terry pointed a finger between us as she raised her eyebrows and struggled to hold in a squeal.

I opened my mouth to say no and confirm that there wasn't anything going on between Poppy and me, but she spoke up before I could stop her.

"Yep. We're dating. Patrick is my boyfriend," Poppy said proudly, smiling so big I worried it would hurt her cheeks.

Fucking Poppy.

"Oh my gosh! Why didn't you say anything?" Terry asked, smacking my arm with her notepad.

"I… Um… Well…"

"He didn't say anything because we've been *secretly* dating," Poppy answered for me, speaking behind her hand as if her voice wasn't loud enough to share the secret she was attempting to hide. "He's best friends with my cousin, Gage, who doesn't know we're dating."

"What?!" Terry exclaimed, drawing the attention of several people at nearby tables. She grinned and scrunched her shoulders, waiting for them to lose interest before speaking again. "I can't believe this! Why haven't I seen you around before?"

"Oh, I live in Coyote Creek, which is about six hours away. We've been doing the whole long-distance thing for a few months now. I decided I was tired of being away from him, so I came into town to spend the holidays with him," Poppy answered as she reached across the table and took my hand, lacing our fingers together. "I just can't get enough of him."

Terry leaned in and spoke behind her hand to Poppy.

"Lock him down while you can. I can't lie and say he hasn't been voted the hottest, most eligible bachelor in Silver Falls. Several women here have had their eye on him and have just been waiting for their chance."

"Well, they'll just have to get in line for the next bachelor because this one is taken."

Poppy grinned at me as we continued to hold hands while I processed what had just happened.

"You better treat her good," Terry warned.

"I wouldn't have it any other way," I replied, speaking only the truth.

Terry took our order and then ran off to the kitchen, no doubt to spread the rumor that Silver Falls' most eligible bachelor was now taken.

<u>Five</u>
Poppy

"Are you sure this is really necessary?" I asked as I followed Patrick through Silver Falls Express as he pushed a shopping cart down one aisle and stopped abruptly in the women's clothing section.

"Yes. It's really necessary given that you didn't bring anything with you besides the clothes on your back, Poppy."

"I wasn't *planning on staying*," I said tightly, forcing a smile when two women looked at us.

Their eyes lit up when they saw Patrick, and then that light diminished when they looked at me. Apparently, good news traveled fast in small towns. I only wish I had taken the time to clean up so I didn't look like Patrick's raggedy girlfriend.

"Well, you were the one who volunteered yourself to be my girlfriend who is staying through the holidays, so you're going to have to live up to that. Your cousin is going to kill me as it is; I don't want to add to it by having you running around wearing my clothes and smelling like me."

"You act like that would be such a bad thing," I muttered, picking at my cuticles to keep from giving dirty looks to the women who were still staring at us.

Patrick looked at me and frowned before looking over to see the two women.

"Six," he said loudly, giving them a nod. They both frowned and tilted their head in confusion. "The record is six orgasms in one night, just in case that's what you ladies were trying to figure out. Our goal is to hit seven tonight, so we're stocking up on supplies so we don't have to leave the cabin for a while." He winked at them and then turned back to face me as my jaw dropped.

"You did *not* just do that," I hissed, looking past him as they grabbed their shopping carts and stormed off.

He shrugged and continued as if he weren't bothered.

"Patrick!" I hissed again, struggling to keep up with him. I finally caught up and walked beside him as I smacked his arm. "You can't go around doing that."

He stopped and turned to face me, his body dangerously close to mine.

"Why not?" he asked, his fingers gently pushing my stomach until my back was against a pole. "You already told Terry that I was your boyfriend. I'm only living up to the part and making sure the people in Silver Falls believe it."

"By making up a lie!"

"Who said it would be a lie?" He licked his lips as his eyes searched my face, quickly noticing the blush that covered my cheeks. "My current record is five in one night, so don't think I'm not some overachiever who isn't ready and willing to beat that."

I swallowed hard, hating how dry my throat suddenly was.

"Let's go get our shopping done so we can visit your cousin and get the ass kicking out of the way." He took a few steps away from me, giving me space to breathe and try to think clearly.

"I don't think it's going to be that bad," I said, following him as he tossed a red hoodie into the cart. "I don't like red."

"Well, it's my favorite color, so you do now," he replied, playfully winking at me. "And yes, it will be that bad."

I pulled the hoodie out of the shopping cart and set it back in the pile it came from, then grabbed a pink one and tossed it in the cart instead.

"You guys are adults now. Do you really think he's going to care if you're *pretending* to date his cousin?"

"I do. Because I nearly beat his ass last year when he started *really* dating my sister."

I scrunched my face, knowing that must have been quite the fight between them.

"Yeah, but sister is different than cousin."

"True. But Gage holds grudges longer than most, and I really don't want to stay on his bad side."

"Well, thankfully, we have plenty of shopping to do here. You said so yourself. We might not even have time to go say hi. What a shame." I shrugged and pulled my mouth into a crooked smile.

"Nice try. We're going to see him and deal with everything today. I hate secrets, so the fewer I have to keep, the better."

"Ugh. Now you tell me," I teased, tossing my head back and groaning.

"Keep it up with that attitude, and there will be a price to pay," he warned, his finger digging into my side where he knew I was ticklish.

"Is that a threat or a promise?" I asked, feeling braver than I was.

I wasn't afraid of Patrick by any means. But that didn't mean that I trusted my heart not to betray me right now, especially since the last thing I needed was any more complications.

<u>Six</u>
Patrick

"No. Bullshit. Undo it," Gage growled, his arms folded over his chest as he looked between Poppy and me with his jaw clenched.

"We can't just *undo it*," Poppy objected, shifting her weight beside me.

His eyes narrowed on her, but he didn't speak. I took a step forward, essentially putting myself in front of Poppy as I stood toe to toe with Gage.

"Really? This is what we're doing?" he asked.

"If that's how you want it to be, then yes. I've said it once; I won't say it again. Protecting Poppy is my only concern, and I don't care what it takes. Stand in my way, and I will make you regret it."

"I don't see why you two have to pretend to be dating," Gage said, looking past me at Poppy. "Why couldn't you just come to me for help?"

"Because you're not being very helpful," my sister, Julie, chided, standing beside him and scowling. "I get that you don't love my brother pretending to be her boyfriend, but you and I both know that she's as safe as she's going to be by staying with him."

"Yeah, but how is that going to work? She goes from being married yesterday to having a fake boyfriend in another town today. You don't think people are going to ask questions?"

"I made a mistake," Poppy said, throwing her hands in the air. "Several, actually, and all of them equally stupid. But there's nothing I can do now unless I leave town and go back to Coyote Creek."

"Do you think it will be safe there, though?" Julie asked softly, clearly on Poppy's side.

"I don't know that anywhere will be safe. They're going to find his body eventually, and when they do, I'm going to be the first person they suspect."

We had arrived at the inn about twenty minutes ago and filled Gage and Julie in on everything after my parents picked up my niece, Daisy, for a playdate at their condo. It was nice having some privacy so we didn't have to worry about her overhearing any of this conversation—the fewer people who knew what Poppy had done, the better.

"Did you tell Terry how long you and Patrick have been dating?" Gage asked, his posture still rigid and tense.

Poppy turned and looked up at me, her face scrunched as she tried to remember.

"You said we had been dating for a few months," I answered softly.

"Shit," Poppy hissed, tipping her head back in frustration.

"It'll be alright," I assured her as I ran my hand across her lower back before pulling it away when Gage's eyes shot daggers at me.

"You said that you got married six months ago in Las Vegas, right?" Julie asked, walking into the open living room and taking a seat on the couch. Poppy and I followed her, with Gage reluctantly trailing behind us.

"Yeah. I was out there with some friends, and he bought us a round. He said he was there for a conference, and then we got talking and found out that we both lived in Coyote Creek. I thought it was strange that I hadn't known who he was, but I also hadn't lived there long. I was new enough for people to know who I was, but I hadn't taken the time to get to know anyone. Anyway, we started drinking, and one thing led to another. Before I knew it, we were saying *I do* and stumbling down the aisle in a rundown building as fake Elvis sang off-key."

"What if you were already dating Patrick before you got married?" Julie said, leaning forward and resting her elbows on her knees. "Maybe you getting married was what temporarily broke you guys up?"

"That could work," I said, raising my eyebrows and nodding.

"Did you ever try to file for divorce?" Gage asked, looking directly at Poppy as he stood next to Julie. He was apparently still too pissed off to take a seat and join us.

"I did, actually. I looked into several options, including annulment. I had paperwork drawn up for the divorce, but he refused to sign it."

"How long ago did you have them drawn up?" I asked, turning to face her.

"About a month after we got married. It was right after the first time he ever laid a hand on me. I decided then that I was done and wanted a divorce. He refused to consider it and shredded the papers."

"Do you still have the contact information for the lawyer?" I asked.

Poppy nodded.

"Yeah, I saved it in case I could get Dale to change his mind. I tried a few times, but each time the punishment got worse, so I just stopped."

"And the bruises on your face and neck?" Gage asked, raising his eyebrows as he stared at Poppy.

"They're from last night," Poppy replied, lowering her eyes and staring at the floor. "He wanted sex, and I said no. He got mad and attacked me. I fought back. The rest is history."

Gage glanced at me and he didn't have to speak for me to know what was going through his mind. I'd had the same thought from the moment I learned about what happened to Poppy. Dale was lucky that Poppy killed him before Gage and I could get our hands on him.

"Okay, so you were attacked last night, and then you drove to Silver Falls this morning to reunite with your boyfriend because you needed somewhere safe to go," Julie said, letting her shoulders fall. "We need to make this story more believable as well as make sure that we cover every base."

"Agreed," I said. "I know that it's Sunday, but do you have a job that you can call and let them know what's going on?"

"Yeah. I work at a salon. I'm scheduled to go in tomorrow."

"Let's call your boss and make sure you let her know that you're scared for your safety," I replied softly, giving her a warm smile.

"Maybe cry if you can," Julie added. "You want them to be able to say that you were upset when you called, so your story is more believable."

"Okay," Poppy agreed, nodding her head before rolling it on her shoulders. She pulled her phone out and swiped the screen until she found the contact she was looking for. Then she pressed send and put the call on speakerphone so we could hear it.

"Hey, Poppy. What's up?" a female voice greeted.

"Hi, Lisa. I'm calling because… I… um…" Poppy paused, and for a second, I thought she was faking emotion until I saw the tears well in her eyes. "I can't come in tomorrow."

"Poppy, what's wrong? Are you okay?" Lisa's tone changed immediately, going from light and carefree to genuinely concerned.

"Dale and I had a fight last night," Poppy said, sniffling as tears ran down her face. "I… he… Oh my God. I'm sorry. I just… I can't come in for a while."

"Are you safe?" Lisa asked, the background noise from a few seconds ago disappearing.

"Yeah. I am now. But I don't know when I'll be able to come back. I'm so sorry. I know I'm letting you down, but

I didn't have a choice but to leave and—"

"Don't say anything else," Lisa warned. "I understand what you're saying. You'll have a spot here *whenever* you decide to return. Take care of yourself, Poppy."

"Thank you, Lisa. I appreciate it."

"Of course. I can only guess what you've been through, so believe me when I say not to let your guard down. Ever. Stay safe, Poppy."

The line went dead before Poppy could say anything more. She set it on the couch beside her and covered her face with her hands as she cried. Julie got up and sat beside Poppy, wrapping her in a hug as she cried.

"I'm sorry, I don't know what happened," Poppy sobbed. "I was fine until I talked to her, and it hit me like a ton of bricks that my life as I knew it was over. The job that I loved so much is gone, all because I was stupid and married some asshole."

"It's okay," Julie assured her. "You've been through a lot. But you're safe now, and that's all that matters. Everything else we can figure out along the way. Is there anyone else you need to call? The more people who know why you left, the better. Gossip will start quickly, especially in a small town. The more you control what they're saying, the less likely they'll consider you a suspect."

"I do some volunteer work at the youth center. I was supposed to help them with an upcoming play this weekend," Poppy answered, wiping her cheeks.

"Well, let's call as many people as we can and share the news about what an asshole Dale was," Julie said, squeezing Poppy in a quick hug before helping her make the phone calls.

I got off the couch and went to the kitchen, needing something to drink while also giving the girls privacy. A few seconds later, Gage joined me.

"I don't like this one bit," he said, his tone still curt.

"There's nothing we can do at this point other than ride this out and see what happens," I replied after taking a long drink of ice-cold water.

"She's my cousin."

"Yeah, and?"

"She's off limits."

"Kinda like how *my sister* was off limits?"

"This isn't the same, and you know it. Things with Julie were different."

"Why? Because it benefited *you*?"

"No, because she is only a few years younger than I am. You're ten years older than Poppy. She was practically a kid when you first met her."

"Teenager," I corrected, though that didn't make it any better. "And in case you haven't noticed, we're both grown adults."

"Don't fucking start with me," Gage warned.

"I could say the same." I set my glass down on the island with more force than I had intended. "You need to get your head straight and stop obsessing over stupid fucking shit.

Your cousin is in trouble and needs our help. Instead of worrying about me possibly fucking her, you should be more concerned with her getting out of the situation she's in. You should be focused on keeping her safe and making sure she doesn't end up going to jail for this, you stupid, self-centered asshole."

Gage pulled back and scoffed, rolling his eyes.

"Don't stand there and act like you don't know that I'm right."

"I do. That's the fucking problem."

"Well, at least we finally agree on something," I replied with a smirk.

"Poppy is my top priority right now. But don't think for a second that I'm just going to look the other way if you try something with her. This isn't like things with Julie and me. Poppy is different. She's had a rough life, and I want to see her get on the right track."

"And you think *I'm* going to hold her back from doing that?"

"No. But I think you sometimes let your cock do the talking for you and Poppy has made enough stupid mistakes as it is."

"Oh. So I would be a mistake?"

"You know what I mean."

"Yeah, you've made your point crystal clear," I replied, pushing past and shoulder-checking him as I stormed out and went back to the living room to check on the girls.

<u>Seven</u>
Poppy

"I can sleep on the couch," I said for what felt like the thousandth time as Patrick narrowed his eyes at me and cocked his head to the side as he leaned against the wall. We got back to his cabin a while ago and were now fighting over where I would sleep. He was just as stubborn as I had remembered.

"And I've already said no. Several times."

"I give up," I muttered, tossing my head back and groaning. "I wouldn't have taken you up on your offer to stay here if I knew that you were going to try to give up your bedroom for me."

"It's seriously not that big of a deal. I sleep on the couch all the time."

"I highly doubt that."

"Okay, so I don't sleep on the couch. But I am more than fine with it and am happy to start tonight."

"Have you seen that storm outside?" I asked, extending my hand to the living room window, which didn't have any curtains and looked like it needed to be replaced. It was old and thin, which meant it would absolutely get freezing cold in here tonight if the power went out.

The wind howled outside as a shiver ran through me.

"What are you going to do when the power goes out?" I continued. "You're going to freeze your balls off."

"My balls and I will be just fine. That's what blankets are for."

I arched an eyebrow and stared at him, ignoring the comment about his balls because those were the *last* thing I needed to think about right now.

"You're not sleeping on the couch," I said bluntly, putting my hands on my hips so he knew I meant business.

His eyes slowly trailed down my body, making note of the gesture as he chewed his lower lip, and his eyes sparkled with mischief.

He pushed off the wall and took a few strides until he was standing right in front of me, violating my space as the light scent of his cologne lingered in the air.

"I think it's cute that you think you can come in here and boss me around," he said, his voice low and deep as butterflies swarmed my stomach. "Make no mistake, Poppy, I decide how things go around here. If I say you're not sleeping on the couch tonight, you're not *fucking sleeping on the couch tonight.*"

"But yet you can?"

He shrugged his shoulders as he shoved his hands into his pockets.

"You should sleep in your bed, Pat. It's more comfortable and I already feel bad enough that I'm crashing here. Please don't make me feel worse that I'm making things hard for you."

"Does it mean that much to you?"

His voice softened as his eyes searched mine.

"Yes," I whispered, my voice struggling to come out. "It would mean a lot to me if you slept in your own bed tonight."

"Fine."

I pulled my head back, trying to hide my confusion but failing. It seemed *way* too easy when he was so adamant about sleeping on the couch a few minutes ago.

"Why are you s—" I started, but stopped when he leaned in and tossed me over his shoulder.

All I could see was his ass as I squealed and tried to see where he was going. It was weird that I didn't immediately flinch or pull away from his touch—instead, I found myself craving more of it. Maybe it was because I had known him for so long and trusted him, or maybe it was because I could tell that he genuinely cared about me and would never hurt me.

"Patrick! What are you doing?"

His hands held the backs of my thighs tighter as he stopped for a moment to open the baby gate at the bottom of the stairs. He walked through, then closed it behind him as the cute Basset Hound puppy whimpered when he was left behind.

"I'll be back to deal with you in a few, Travis," he said over his shoulder to the dog.

"Seriously, what are you doing? Put me down," I warned, though I couldn't stop laughing.

He stepped into the room and deposited me gently on a plush king-sized bed before stepping back and allowing his eyes to roam my body once more.

"I thought I made myself clear," he said, taking a few steps back as he grabbed his hoodie from the back and pulled it over his head. The fabric caught on his t-shirt underneath, pulling it up with it and showing a sliver of the most beautifully sculpted abs I had ever seen. "You're not sleeping on the couch. Since you said it means so much to you that *I* don't sleep on the couch, the only solution to our problem is that we share my bed."

"What?" I asked, leaning forward as I hung onto his words and my jaw dropped. "You've got to be kidding me."

"Nope."

"But we can't share a bed," I said with a nervous laugh.

"Why not?"

"Well… I ummm… There's… Ummm… My cousin would be *pissed* if he found out," I finally blurted out, hating that I didn't have a good excuse for not wanting to sleep in his bed other than because I wasn't sure I could stop myself from trying to touch him.

"I hate to break it to you, but I don't give a flying fuck what *your cousin* thinks. Gage is the least of my concerns right now."

"Why is that?" I asked dumbly. It was obvious, but for whatever reason, I still wanted to hear him say it. *I needed to hear him say it.*

"Because keeping you safe is the only thing I'm worried about right now. Gage can be mad if he wants to. But I'll be damned if I let anything happen to you while you're staying with me. That includes allowing you to sleep on a shitty couch in a cold living room."

I nodded and sat on my hands to keep from fidgeting. I couldn't remember the last time a guy had cared so much about my well-being. Scratch that—I couldn't remember the last time *anyone* cared at all about my well-being.

"I need to go get Travis settled for the night. Feel free to set up whatever you need in the bathroom. We'll do laundry in the morning so you'll have clean clothes to wear, but for the time being, help yourself to anything you want in my closet."

He smiled warmly and walked out of the room, leaving me sitting there as I tried to process how I had gotten myself stuck with being taken care of by the most caring man in the world.

Eight
Patrick

After I got Travis situated and secured in his kennel, I headed back upstairs for the night. Having a puppy was fun, but it was seriously what I expected to be the equivalent of having a human child. He couldn't be left alone more than a few minutes without me having to worry that he was destroying something. His current obsession was chewing anything and everything he could get his paws on, which was why I had waited to buy new furniture. I didn't want to get anything new until he was out of this phase, although I wasn't sure it would pass anytime soon.

When I walked into the bedroom, I stopped in my tracks and froze as I saw Poppy sitting on the bed wearing one of my older t-shirts and rubbing the lotion she bought earlier along her arms. It was one of my favorite shirts, which explained why it was old and worn out. However, I suddenly loved it for different reasons—none of which had anything to do with the fact that it was practically transparent, and I could see she wasn't wearing a bra.

"I hope it's okay I borrowed this," she said, tugging the fabric away from her body as she looked up at me with those beautiful blue eyes. "It just looked so comfy."

"Of course. I want you to feel comfortable here, so help yourself to whatever you want."

Like my cock, if you want it.

"I can't say it enough, but thank you again for letting me stay here. I know this day has been wild and not what anyone expected, but I appreciate your grace and generosity with everything."

"You don't need to thank me, Poppy. I would much rather have you stay with me so I can make sure you're okay than to have you out on your own and having to worry about whether you're safe."

She squirted some lotion into her hand before setting the bottle of lotion on the nightstand and turning to face me.

"You would be worried about me?"

"Of course I would. Why wouldn't I be?"

She shrugged and let out a soft sigh.

"I don't know. I can't remember the last time anyone worried about me," she replied quietly as she applied the lotion to her legs.

"Well, then I would say you've been hanging out with the wrong people."

"You could say that again. But then again, that *is* the story of my life, so why change now?"

She laughed, but I just stared at her, hating that she felt that way about herself.

"You're worth caring about, Poppy," I said, feeling a tightness in my chest.

"You have to say that because you're my cousin's best friend, but thank you for the sentiment."

"I probably *shouldn't* be saying it because you're my best friend's cousin, but I don't care."

"So you've said."

I nodded and pressed my lips together to keep from saying anything more as she ran her hands along the tops of her thighs, rubbing the lotion in. I didn't want to be a pervert and look, but it was nearly impossible not to with the amount of skin showing from under the bottom of my t-shirt. I gulped and swallowed hard, forcing myself to look the other way when I realized that the only thing Poppy was wearing was my t-shirt and a pair of black panties.

****

After a restless night, I got up and took a shower, being quiet to keep from waking Poppy. She had seemed just as restless, but I tried not to focus on that as the t-shirt she was wearing continued to rise throughout the night. I had the perfect view of her ass and had to keep my hands to myself, which left me feeling horny and frustrated.

I grabbed the bottle of body wash from the shelf and squirted some into my hand as I enjoyed the spray of hot water across my back. My cock was hard and aching as I gripped it, sliding my hand up and down the shaft as I closed my eyes.

Visions of Poppy's perky tits in my t-shirt entered my mind, making my dick harder as I thought about sucking her hard nipples and sliding my hand inside her panties. Her big, plump ass looked amazing in those panties, but I could imagine how fantastic it would look bouncing over my cock as she rode me.

I moaned and tipped my head back as I stroked harder, the mere thought of fucking Poppy nearly sending me over the edge. While she was off limits and my focus needed to stay on protecting her, I couldn't help but think about how good it would feel to have her lips wrapped around my cock as she took me to the back of her throat.

"Fuck, Poppy," I whispered, my balls beginning to tighten as I got closer.

Just then, a soft noise startled me, making my eyes fly open. My heart stammered in my chest as I looked up and caught Poppy standing in the doorway, watching me jack off.

While I loved the large walk-in shower with the full-length glass door that I added when I moved in, I never in a million years would have thought that my best friend's cousin would be watching me masturbate through it.

Nine
Poppy

Patrick didn't just have a big dick—he had a thick, veiny cock that I wanted nothing more than to suck. My panties were soaked as I watched him masturbate in the shower. I was tempted to reach down and get myself off, but the moment he opened his eyes and saw me, I froze.

He stood under the water, still grabbing his cock as his jaw tightened and he stared at me. I opened my mouth to speak, but my throat was too dry to get any words out. I knew I should have turned around and walked out the second I heard the shower was on, but my curiosity got the best of me—*story of my life*.

"I'm sorry," I rushed out, spinning on my heel to make a beeline out of there.

But before I could leave, he stopped me.

"Poppy," he said, his voice coarse and demanding. "What are you doing in here?"

I kept my back to him, not trusting myself to turn around and *not* invite myself to join him in the shower.

"I needed to pee," I lied, speaking loud enough for him to hear me over the water.

"Go ahead. The toilet is free."

I spun around, my eyes wild as I stared at him. He couldn't possibly be serious.

"What? I can't pee in here."

"Why not?" he asked as he lazily slid his hand up his shaft.

I struggled to keep my eyes on his face and not allow them to trail down to where they wanted to look instead. *That thing was HUGE.*

"Because that would be weird. I can't let you watch me pee."

"Yet you're standing there watching me jack off," he said simply as if this wasn't the most inappropriate thing in the world to be happening right now.

"I didn't know you would be in here… doing that…"

"Yet you didn't leave when you saw what I was doing."

He licked his lips as our gazes stayed locked on each other.

"I'm going to finish in here. You're welcome to use this bathroom, or you can use the one downstairs."

I nodded, unsure of what to do, mainly because *peeing* wasn't what I needed right now.

"Okay. Yeah. Umm… Thanks."

He closed his eyes and let his head fall back the way it was when I first walked in.

"Oh, and Poppy?" he said, pulling my attention back to him.

"Yeah?"

"If you're going to stand there and watch me jack off, you might as well join me in the shower. You'll get a better view of the show."

My cheeks flushed with heat as I considered his offer. It wasn't like Patrick and I hadn't felt the chemistry between us yesterday. It sizzled hotter than I had ever felt with anyone before, so it wasn't surprising that we would be so quick to act on it, even if we both had been trying to deny it was there.

I pulled my shoulders back and walked over to the shower door with more confidence than I'd ever had before. His eyes fluttered open as a huge smile spread across his cheeks. He reached forward and slid the door open, waiting for me to step inside before pulling it closed.

The hot water sprayed my skin as he stepped back and watched as it soaked the t-shirt, making it even more see-through than it already was. The fabric clung to my skin as I watched him touch himself, the desire to feel him in *my hand* almost too much to bear.

I stepped forward, my eyes on his as I reached down and brushed my fingers against the tip of his cock. He hissed and chewed his lower lip as he continued to watch me. I pulled the hair tie off my wrist and secured my hair on top of my head before I lowered myself to my knees and grabbed his cock. He moved his hand out of the way, allowing me full access as he looked down, his rapt attention solely on me as he watched as I slid him into my mouth and took him all the way to the back of my throat.

I gagged slightly, opening my mouth wider and unclenching my jaw as I slowly pulled him out and flicked the head with my tongue. He was heavy in my hand, which made my pussy ache with need as I imagined him fucking me. He was so hard, and I could tell he had been close to coming before he caught me watching.

"Fuck, Poppy," he moaned, letting out a ragged breath as his hand wrapped around the back of my head and gently guided me as I bobbed up and down, increasing the speed as I hollowed out my cheeks and sucked harder. "I'm close. You better stop if you don't—"

Before he could finish his sentence, I grabbed the part of his shaft that didn't fit in my mouth and stroked it as I continued sucking, loving it the second I felt ropes of cum shoot down the back of my throat. He grunted and wrapped my hair tightly around his fist as he came. Once he was finished, I slowly pulled away, gently stroking his cock as I stared up at him. He let go of my hair and tenderly brushed his fingers across my cheek.

"I knew you would be trouble," he said softly as he stared at me.

He reached down and helped me up, his eyes catching on the t-shirt again.

"While I love this on you, it needs to come off."

I nodded as he took a few steps, forcing me out of the water as he shielded it with his back. He lifted the bottom of the shirt and slowly pulled it up and over my head, letting it fall with a heavy thud as it landed beside us.

My body hummed with need as his fingers lightly trailed over my skin. I wanted him to touch me and tease me the way I knew only he could. Hell, he hadn't even *touched* me yet, and I was about to come from the heated look he gave me.

"I want to eat your pussy and have you come on my face, but that's a little hard to do in here," he said softly. "So why don't we get cleaned up so I can go make a mess of you in the bedroom?"

A whoosh of air escaped my parted lips as every nerve in my body lit on fire from the arousal rushing through me. I nodded, the movement stopping abruptly as he leaned in and lowered his lips to mine, devouring them in a kiss. It wasn't gentle or soft—it was filled with a needy hunger for more of each other.

I locked my arms around his neck and parted my lips, allowing him more access. His hands slid down my sides and then dipped down to grab my ass. He lifted me to his hips effortlessly, and I broke the kiss and gasped when I felt his erection. *Fuck. I thought I just took care of that.*

"I have the gift that keeps on giving," he teased, somehow reading my mind.

"Well, I hate to break it to you, but you're a little early. It's still three weeks until Christmas."

"Yeah, and it's not just the *stockings* that are hung."

"You could say that again," I replied with a giggle as he shifted so his cock pressed right against my entrance.

"Shower first, fun after," he said, giving me a look.

I sighed heavily, more for dramatic effect as I carefully slid down his body and stood on my own so we could actually shower together.

<u>Ten</u>
Patrick

I leaned in closer, pinning Poppy to the bed with the weight of my body as I settled between her thighs. Her pussy was slick with arousal, begging me to do all of the things I wanted to do to bring her to climax. The problem was that I didn't want her to just come—I wanted her to come repeatedly and take pride in knowing that *I* brought her that pleasure.

"Are you sure this is what you want?" I asked, lifting my head to look at her.

While we had already talked about how much she wanted me to fuck her and eat her pussy, I wasn't going to jump into anything without making sure she still wanted to. Consent wasn't something I would overlook, especially given the bullshit her husband tried with her.

She nodded her head and then let it fall back on the pillow without answering me.

I grabbed her thighs, getting her attention as I raised an eyebrow at her.

"I need to hear you say it."

"Yes, Pat. I want you to eat my pussy and make me come on your face."

Fuck. Just hearing her say that had my dick hardening again.

"Good girl," I growled before I lowered my head and swiped my tongue along her slit, loving the way she gasped before reaching down and locking her fingers in my hair.

Her skin smelled like the body wash she used in the shower, and the light scent of raspberries was driving me wild. It was like literally eating forbidden fruit, and I loved every second of it.

I pulled her clit between my lips and sucked as I slid two fingers inside of her. The way her pussy clenched around them made my cock ache as I imagined how tight she would grip it. Just the thought of coming inside of her had me thrusting my fingers faster as I sucked harder, desperate to give her the relief I knew she needed.

"Fuck!" she gasped, nearly bucking off the bed as I held onto her, maintaining the pace and rhythm until she shuddered around me.

Once I knew she was done, I slowly pulled away, releasing my fingers from her pussy before licking her arousal from them. She watched with rapt fascination as I cleaned them, taking my time.

"You taste fucking amazing," I said as I climbed up the bed and laid next to her.

We hadn't bothered getting dressed after the shower, which meant my cock was on full display as my erection jutted up to my stomach and a dot of precum glistened at the tip.

"You're a little too good at what you just did," she teased. "I don't think I've ever come that fast or that hard."

"Well, I aim to please," I replied, wiggling my eyebrows.

"If that's the case, then I would love some of that cock." She pointed to it and licked her lips.

"How do you want it?"

"However you want to do it is fine with me."

"Nope. Not happening."

"What do you mean, *not happening*? I thought you just said you aimed to please. I don't want to sound like a bitch, but I'll totally one-star you…"

I grinned, loving how adorable and feisty she was.

"I mean that you need to tell me what *you* want, Poppy. I'm not the kind of man who is just going to do what I want, how I want, or when I want. So, I'll ask you again—how do you want it?"

She chewed her lip as she watched me, and it killed me not knowing what she was thinking.

"I can take you from behind, you can ride me, we can do it missionary style, I can bend you into a pretzel and jackhammer the fuck out of you… Tell me what you like, Poppy. What will bring you the most pleasure?"

She glanced down at my cock as I lazily stroked it.

"I don't know. I want all of that and more." She laughed and covered her mouth as if she couldn't believe the words had come out of it. "Maybe we can start with the pretzel thing?"

I nodded, fully on board with doing whatever she wanted to do.

"Is that what you want?"

"Yes. I want you to fold me in weird ways and then fuck me hard and rough."

"You got it." I grinned at her before I leaned over and pressed my lips against hers, loving how quickly her body responded to me.

Her legs parted, inviting me in as I laid on top of her, holding as much of my weight as I could so I didn't smother her. She parted her lips, giving my tongue access as my hands explored her body. Her fingers reached down and grabbed my cock, stroking it the best she could in the cramped space between us.

I didn't want to stop, but I also wasn't going to be able to go that long without being inside of her and I needed to grab a condom. I pulled away slowly, watching as she continued to stroke my cock. Her hands felt like magic as she worked me up without sending me over the edge. I reached into the nightstand, grabbed a condom, and put it on while she laid back and watched me.

"Are you ready?" I asked, loving her naked body spread out beneath me.

"Yes. Please fuck me already, Pat," she said, letting out a soft moan as I lined my cock up at her entrance.

"I want to start slowly before I fuck you hard and rough," I explained, pressing a little more until my cock parted her lips and slid inside her warm pussy.

"Fuck," she cried out, letting a heavy breath escape. "That feels so good."

"You're so fucking tight," I replied, my jaw clenched as I tried not to blow my load right away. I knew she would be tight, but I hadn't expected this tight.

She lifted her hips, allowing me to slide further inside of her until I couldn't go any deeper. She opened her eyes and watched me as she rubbed her hands over her breasts, playing with her nipples while I slowly pulled out and slid back inside of her.

"You're gonna make me come if you don't stop doing that," she warned.

All I heard was a challenge to make her come again.

I leaned forward and nudged her hand out of the way as I replaced it with my mouth, pulling a puckered nipple in between my lips and sucking. She cried out as her nails scratched along my back, leaving the perfect trail of pain and pleasure. I pulled out and then slammed back into her, loving the way she moaned and tightened around me.

While I wanted to make her into a pretzel and fuck her, I was enjoying this too much to stop. I pulled out and entered her again a few more times, thrusting harder with each stroke. She wrapped her fingers in my hair as I moved to her other nipple and sucked while I thrusted hard and fast, making sure to rub her clit with each thrust.

"Fuck. Fuck. Fuck. FUUCCCKKKK," she screamed, her body trembling beneath me as I brought her to climax again.

She was panting and laid limp on the bed by the time I pulled out and disposed of the condom after I came with her. Her body was a fucking wonderland, and I was ready to spend the holidays there.

"We didn't get to do it pretzel style, but that was the best fucking sex I've ever had," she replied, still slightly breathless. "I can't believe you made me come twice already."

"I wasn't kidding when I said my record was six times in a night,' I teased.

"Stop it, I don't want to hear about you fucking other girls." She swatted at my chest as I laid down beside her.

"I'm just kidding. I've never kept track of it before. But I am curious to see how many I can get out of you. Your body responds so easily to my touch; it makes me want to see what else it likes."

"That's because I trust you and you make me feel safe," she whispered, her face quickly turning white as she realized what she had said.

She tried to hide her face behind her arms, but I gently reached over and covered her hands with mine, lowering them to rest against her chest.

"I will never take that trust for granted, Poppy. I want you to *always* feel safe with me. I take that very seriously and will never intentionally do anything to hurt you. It's okay to let yourself feel this way with me. No matter what happens, I've got you."

She nodded as a stray tear slid down her cheek before she quickly blinked the rest away.

Eleven
Poppy

It hadn't even been a full forty-eight hours of me staying with Patrick, and we already had sex. Not that I was upset about that, because I wasn't. Sex with Pat was phenomenal and better than anything I'd ever had before, but I wasn't sure he felt the same way. While he was still being his same friendly self, I could sense the barrier he was trying to put up between us. We had the opportunity to have sex several times already this morning, and he seemed to avoid all of them. He seemed to thoroughly enjoy himself last night, which left me wondering if his avoidance of me had something to do with my cousin and his warning to stay away from me.

I was sitting in the kitchen at the table when he came in and arched an eyebrow at me.

"What are you eating?" he asked.

"Breakfast," I replied, showing him the bag of mini Oreos.

"That's breakfast?"

"Yep. Breakfast of champions."

He shook his head and walked to the stove, where he

grabbed a few pans and set them on the burners.

"That's not breakfast," he countered.

"Sure it is." I shrugged, popping another tiny cookie into my mouth and grinning at him.

"There's nothing nutritious about that. How are you supposed to have energy for the day if you eat junk food for breakfast?"

"I don't know." I laughed. "I guess I never really gave it much thought. I usually just drink coffee and go about my day. This is a big step for me because I rarely eat in the morning."

"Why not?"

"I'm not usually hungry. I've never been a big breakfast person. It used to drive my parents crazy, but then again, there wasn't much about me that *didn't* drive them mad."

"Well, it's a little late for breakfast, but I'm going to make it anyway. Are there any breakfast foods you like?"

"Oh, there's plenty," I said as I got up and threw my empty bag in the trash. "I love breakfast foods, I just don't eat them in the morning."

"Fair enough," he replied as he opened the refrigerator and started pulling food out. "Does scrambled eggs and sausage sound okay?"

"It sounds delicious, but really, you don't have to cook for me. I'm not that hungry in the morning."

He looked around me to see the clock on the stove as he set a carton of eggs on the counter.

"It's after eleven, which means it's almost lunch time. So, like it or not—I'm feeding you."

I exhaled heavily, making sure to roll my eyes so he knew how dramatic I was being.

"Fine. If you insist."

Just when I thought I finally had the upper hand, he walked in front of me, placing the pack of sausage down beside the eggs. He gently pinched my chin between his fingers as his heated gaze penetrated mine.

"Good girl," he murmured, making sure my body felt the weight of his words.

My thighs clenched in response, attempting to dull the ache that was sure to start building.

"What do you need help with?" I asked once he stepped away, and I was able to clear the fog from my head.

"Nothing. I've got it, but thank you. You're welcome to find something for us to watch on TV if you want to."

I nodded and made my way into the living room, smiling at the cutest little puppy until I stopped in my tracks. The Bassett hound looked up at me from its spot on the couch, the remote for the TV tucked firmly between its paws.

"Umm…." I said, unsure of how to tell him his dog had eaten a good chunk of the remote.

"What's wrong?"

"It seems your dog got to the remote before I could."

I scrunched my face as he set the spatula down on the

counter and tipped his head back in frustration.

"Fucking, Travis," he muttered as he walked around the island that separated the living room from the kitchen and stood beside me. "Are you kidding me?"

Travis whined as he looked up at us with the saddest eyes I had ever seen.

"Aww," I whispered, trying my best not to laugh.

"Nope. Don't you dare sympathize with this *monster*." He reached down and grabbed the remote from Travis, holding it away from him as slobber dripped from the end of it. "You're *this* close to being a stray. I swear to God, if you eat one more thing…"

"I take it he does this often?"

Patrick looked at me while the remote still dangled between his fingers.

"*He* is the reason I haven't bought new furniture. I have yet to find something he doesn't chew on and destroy."

I pressed my lips together to keep from laughing as he shook his head and grabbed a few tissues to wipe off the remote.

"Puppies do that," I offered softly, fighting the urge to scratch Travis's tummy as he rolled onto his back and looked at us.

"So I'm finding out."

"You didn't know this in advance?"

"In all fairness, I'm not a dog person."

"Why did you get a puppy then?"

"My niece Daisy wanted one, and I couldn't say no. Her mom wouldn't let her have one, so I was the stupid one who volunteered to get one instead. She's supposed to come by and help with him, but they've been busy. Given how much work he is, I kinda understand now why my sister was against it."

"I see," I said, nodding my head. "Well, he seems fairly young. How old is he?"

"I got him when he was ten weeks old, and I've had him for a few months, I think?" He scratched his head as he tried to remember.

"Well, the nice thing is that he's still trainable. You just have to work with him, but you should be able to break some of these bad habits."

"You really think there's hope for him?" Pat arched an eyebrow in question.

"If I could turn my life around, there's no doubt he can turn his around too," I teased.

I caught a glimpse of Patrick as his jaw tightened before he walked off and resumed cooking. I knew he hated it when I said stuff like that, but if he knew the things I had done in my life, he wouldn't want anything to do with me.

58

Twelve
Poppy

The sun peeked through the sheer curtains, greeting me as I opened my eyes. The sound of my phone ringing on the nightstand beside me startled me. I reached over and grabbed it, my heart sinking when I saw the phone number. Although the phone number was unknown, the area code was for Coyote Creek.

"Hello," I answered, trying to keep my voice steady so the panic rising inside of me didn't come through.

"Hello. May I please speak with Poppy Grant?" a male voice asked.

"Yes. This is she."

"Mrs. Grant, this is Detective Gibson from the Coyote Creek Sheriff's Department."

I stayed silent and waited for him to tell me what he was calling for. When he didn't continue, I swallowed down the rising bile and forced myself to speak.

"How can I help you?" I asked, pulling my shoulders back as I took slow, calming breaths.

"The reason for my phone call today is that we have not been able to reach your husband, Sheriff Hudson. Do you know of his whereabouts?"

"I do not," I replied right as Patrick walked into the room. I lifted my finger to my lips, asking him to be quiet as he furrowed his brow and folded his arms over his chest.

"When was the last time you saw him?" Detective Gibson pressed, pulling my attention back to the phone call.

"I last saw my husband a few nights ago. We had a fight, and I left after he assaulted me."

"Where did you go?"

I paused for a second, hoping that I didn't dig myself into a hole I couldn't get out of.

"I just took off, walking until I reached the highway. I saw a truck headed west, so I flagged it down and asked for a ride," I lied, but it was the easiest way to get around the fact that I took Dale's car and drove with him in the trunk to Silver Falls. There wouldn't be any way for them to verify my story if I didn't get any contact information for the trucker I supposedly got a ride from, and thanks to the snowstorm that had blown in, the traffic cameras wouldn't have caught anything either.

"Where are you now?"

"I'm sorry?" I felt my skin prickle as I considered whether to share this information with him. I didn't know if I was required to by law or if they could throw me in jail for failure to cooperate.

"Where are you now, Mrs. Grant?" he repeated sternly.

"I'm staying with a friend in Silver Falls," I answered, feeling the blood drain from my face.

"How long have you been there?"

"Since Sunday morning."

"What is the name of the friend you're staying with?"

"I'm sorry, but I don't understand how this information is related to discovering my husband's whereabouts," I replied, struggling to hold onto the ounce of courage I felt.

The detective on the other end of the line sighed heavily before he answered.

"The FBI is investigating your husband. They've discovered a large offshore bank account with you listed as the sole beneficiary. So, I'm going to ask you one more time, what is the name of the friend you are staying with?"

I swallowed hard, everything inside of me screaming danger as I processed the information.

"Patrick Kennedy," I answered. "I'm staying with my ex-boyfriend, Patrick Kennedy."

"Thank you. Please note that while we cannot require you to return to Coyote Creek, we have obtained a search warrant that will be executed. This gives us permission to enter your home and search it without you being present," he warned before hanging up.

I let the phone fall to my lap as my lip trembled. Patrick rushed over and stood beside me, rubbing his hand soothingly up and down my back.

"What was that all about?" he asked.

I blinked a few times to get myself to focus as I looked up at him.

"The FBI is investigating Dale, and apparently, there's an offshore account with a large sum of money. They said that I'm the sole beneficiary."

"Did you know about that account?"

"No," I whispered, bringing my hands up to my face. "But this is bad, Pat. Like, really, really bad."

"They can't prove you had anything to do with it if you didn't even know it existed until now," he assured me. "It'll be fine. I promise."

"No! You don't get it," I said, getting off the bed and standing in front of him. "I got fired from my last job for embezzlement. I have a record and served a few months in jail. There's no way they're going to overlook that, especially when I've only been married to Dale for *six months*. Don't you see how this is going to look?"

He worked his jaw back and forth as he studied me.

"I warned you," I said with a sob. "I'm not the person you think I am. I've done terrible things and have gotten involved with the wrong people. All I'm going to do is bring trouble to your life, and you don't need that."

"Stop it," he demanded as he wrapped his arms around me and held me against his chest. "We'll figure this out."

Thirteen
Patrick

"Can they legally do that?" Julie asked as we sat on the couch at the inn, filling her and Gage in on what was happening.

"We looked it up, and online it says that they can enter the house without our permission if they have a search warrant, which he said they did," Poppy answered.

"Are they going to find anything incriminating against you in the house?" Gage asked, studying Poppy with a look I wanted to smack off his face. She'd been through a lot already; she didn't need his judgmental attitude on top of everything else.

"No. I don't think so," Poppy answered. "I mean, it's public record that I did time for embezzlement. They're going to find that out the second they pull up my information. But I left that life behind when I moved to Coyote Creek to start over. There shouldn't be anything in the house that could make me look bad, unless Dale had something to do with it."

"Setting up an offshore account with you as the sole beneficiary definitely doesn't look good," Gage replied, his attitude softening some.

"I know. Unfortunately, I have no idea what that account is for or why he listed me as the beneficiary. I've spent the majority of my time trying to figure out how to divorce him, not get to know him. It wasn't like we were madly in love, and he wanted to make sure I was taken care of if anything ever happened to him."

"This whole thing sounds fishy," Julie said, scrunching her nose.

"I agree. But, this could work in our favor," I said, leaning forward and resting my elbows on my knees.

"How so?" Gage asked.

"Maybe it wasn't coincidental that you guys met in Vegas. What if he searched you out? Not only that, but he's apparently involved in something illegal with that offshore account. Who's to say that they'll even suspect Poppy of murdering him? If he was in with the wrong people, his death could be considered an act of retaliation for messing something up."

"I guess there's nothing we can do right now other than wait and see what happens," Poppy said, looking defeated and scared.

I leaned back and wrapped my arm around her shoulders as I pulled her into my side and kissed her temple. It took a split second for me to realize what I had just done in front of her cousin. I felt Poppy relax in my arms, but that was quickly replaced when her body went rigid the moment Gage spoke.

"I fucking knew it," he muttered, shaking his head as he stared at us. "It hasn't even been a *week,* and you couldn't keep your dick in your fucking pants."

Fourteen
Poppy

"How's your eye?" I asked as I stood next to Patrick, examining the bruise.

I winced as I looked at it, hating that I was the one who had given it to him. He'd caught me by surprise last night while I was making dinner, and the touch of his hand on my waist triggered a reaction that I couldn't control. I had been so used to Dale doing that to me that I didn't even think before I swung around and punched him.

"I'm fine. Please stop worrying about it. Besides, it's nice to know that your aim is better than your cousin's. Now I'll have something new to make fun of him for."

I hadn't heard from Gage or Julie, but we all agreed that I would call if we needed anything. Otherwise, we would give each other space. It was best for everyone if we let things between the guys settle a bit before spending any more time together. The last thing I wanted was for a fight to come between them, especially this close to Christmas. I wanted to keep whatever peace I could, which meant giving Gage time to process the news that something had happened between Patrick and me.

I sat on the couch and stared out the window, watching the snow fall while he sat beside me, resting as he closed his eyes. It was a calm day, which was nice, given that we seemed to have missed the brutal storm predicted to hit Silver Falls a few days ago. I hadn't kept up with the news to see if there had been any changes, but I was thankful that I could still leave town if I needed to. With the way things were going between Patrick and Gage, I was starting to worry that I would.

Suddenly, there was a knock on the front door, spurring Travis into action as he barked and howled at it. Patrick got up and opened the door, glancing nervously at me as two police officers stood outside.

"May I help you?" Pat asked, keeping the door open enough for me to hear the conversation without allowing them to see me.

"We are looking for Poppy Grant. We have a source that confirmed she was staying here."

Patrick nodded and stepped to the side as I stood up. I lowered my hands to my sides to keep from fidgeting as I walked over and joined them.

"That's me," I said softly, trying to force myself not to appear weak.

The two officers exchanged a look before one nodded, and the other looked at me with a solemn expression.

"Mrs. Grant, your husband is dead. We regret to inform you that we found his body last night in a vehicle registered to him that had washed ashore in the river."

I gasped, not even attempting to fake a reaction. My hands

clasped over my mouth as tears stung my eyes. While I knew that *I* had killed Dale, it felt very different to hear someone else say the words.

"What?" I stammered as I struggled to stay composed. Out of all of the times to have an emotional breakdown over what had happened, this was the absolute worst time for one. "What are you talking about?"

Patrick moved out of the way, inviting the officers inside before closing the door behind them. The female officer approached me calmly, her face soft and comforting.

"We were called out to investigate a car that had washed ashore in the river," she explained again. "Inside the car, we found the body of Dale Hudson. Silver Falls Police Department had been made aware of a missing person alert from Coyote Creek when Sheriff Hudson hadn't been seen in a few days. I'm very sorry to deliver this news to you."

I shook my head as I felt my legs tremble before I dropped to the ground and cried. I wasn't necessarily crying over Dale or the fact that I had murdered him. I was crying because it was real. Not only had I killed him, I also stopped the cycle of abuse from ever happening again. I was finally free, and there was nothing he could do to hurt me anymore. But that didn't make me feel any better about knowing that I had taken a life.

The police officer knelt beside me and offered me her hand as Patrick helped me to my feet. I had forgotten that I hadn't done anything to hide the bruises on my neck from where Dale tried to strangle me, but the second the officer spotted them, I felt the tension in the room shift.

She immediately stood up, her hand flew to her holster, and

she looked between Patrick and me as if that would give her the answer she was looking for.

"It's not what you think," I explained, letting my fingers trail over the bruises as I sniffled. "He didn't do this to me."

"Would you like to tell me who did?" the officer asked politely, still side-eying Patrick. He took a cautious step back, making sure to give me enough space so it didn't look like he was controlling me, without being too far in case I needed him. I knew she was probably also questioning the black eye he was sporting, thanks to me.

I knew this was my chance to give them my side of the story. If I wanted them to rule me out as a person of interest, I needed to make sure they knew what exactly I had been running from the night I escaped Dale.

"My husband," I replied, looking the female officer in the eyes. "Sheriff Hudson constantly abused me during the six months we were married. I tried several times to leave him and asked for a divorce, but he refused. The last attack happened several nights ago. I left town and came here. I've been staying with my ex—now current boyfriend, since then."

I paused for a moment, looking at Patrick before I continued.

"His black eye is from me," I admitted, nodding to Pat. "He startled me, and my instinct was to protect myself, so I punched him."

A look of understanding flashed across the female cop's face as she pressed her mouth into a soft smile and gave me a single nod.

"Did you ever go to the police to file a restraining order or to report the abuse?" the male officer asked.

I nodded and took a deep breath, letting it out slowly.

"I tried everything I could think of, but I'm sure you can understand how difficult it was to convince anyone in a small town that their beloved sheriff was abusing his wife. I wasn't able to get the assistance or protection that I needed, so I left."

"When was the last time you saw your husband?" the male officer pressed as he pulled out a notepad and jotted down something.

"He was still inside the house when I left Saturday night. I don't know what happened after that. I got a phone call earlier from Detective Gibson of the Coyote Creek Sheriff's Department, stating they were trying to locate him."

"We spoke with Detective Gibson as well," the female officer confirmed. "It was how we received the information about your whereabouts. We contacted them once we identified the body, since there was a missing person alert."

"So, what happens now?" Patrick asked, wrapping a protective arm around me as I leaned into him.

"The body has been taken to the local morgue, where they will perform a full autopsy at the request of the medical examiner. After that is complete, you can discuss transportation options with the funeral home if you would like to have his body transported back to Coyote Creek for burial," the male officer explained as he put his notepad and pen away before pulling a business card out of his pocket. "This is the information for the funeral home in Silver Falls."

Patrick took the card and put it in his pocket without letting go of me.

"Would you like to file a police report for the attack that happened the night you left?" the female officer asked as she looked from me to the male officer.

"With Silver Falls, or do you mean back in Coyote Creek?"

"In Silver Falls."

"Is it necessary? I mean, it's not like they can do anything to him now."

"It's absolutely your decision. But I've learned that it's never too late to say something. Just because we can't arrest him for what he did doesn't mean we have to ignore what happened. People deserve to know the truth about who he was and what he was capable of."

There was something that felt off about what she was asking, but I couldn't put my finger on what it was. I studied her for a few minutes until I recognized the look in her eye. The sadness that clouded her blue eyes as she struggled to hide it from me. It was the same look I had after he hit me the first time. It never went away.

"You didn't get to report yours," I whispered.

She shook her head and pressed her lips together.

"I wish I would have, because maybe if I would have told someone what was happening, they would have stopped him. Instead, I packed my bags and moved to Silver Falls, leaving Coyote Creek behind."

My heart skipped a beat as I processed her words. Dale had hurt her, too.

"You weren't the first woman he put his hands on, but you will be the last. I didn't have the courage to report it when it happened to me, but I would like to help you do what I couldn't."

"Okay. Tell me what we need to do," I said, as a wave of emotions washed over me.

72

Fifteen
Patrick

The day had been long, but I couldn't focus on anything other than Poppy and how she was doing with everything. I had tried to give her space because I wasn't sure what she needed, but when I saw her sitting on the couch with her knees pulled to her chest as she tried to hide her tears from me, I decided that was enough. She was mine to take care of, and I was going to do just that.

"I got you," I said softly as I sat beside her and wrapped my arms around her. She didn't fight me as she leaned into my touch and cried harder. "Whatever you need, I've got you."

I held Poppy while she cried, but I couldn't deny that it changed something deep inside of me. Helping Poppy was easy. She was my best friend's cousin, which made her practically family. But the more time I spent with her and the deeper I got involved with everything, the more I realized I was in way over my head. We had only slept together once, so it wasn't like we were dating. I had no claim to her, even if I wanted to. She was still married—or widowed if we were being technical.

Her body trembled against mine as she wept, but I didn't ask any questions until she was ready. A few minutes later, she pulled away and wiped at her eyes with the sleeves of her hoodie before looking at me.

"I killed my husband," she said, choking back a sob as a tear ran down her face. "I'm a murderer."

"You're not a murderer, Poppy," I assured her, making sure she saw the truth in my eyes. "You protected yourself the only way you could. That's different and no one can blame you for what you did."

"I took a life, Pat. I killed him."

"I know, baby. I know. But you were only protecting yourself."

"What kind of terrible person am I that I could just take a life and then not think twice about it as I tried to get rid of his body? Who does that? Why didn't I call the police and tell them what happened? I didn't have to kill him—I could have—"

"You know what would have happened if you called the police. They would have come out and taken his side. You know they wouldn't have gone against the sheriff. You did what you had to do, Poppy, and I will die on that hill."

"You don't have to say that to make me feel better. Maybe I deserve to feel like this. Maybe this is my karma for what I did."

"I will never try to tell you how to feel about *anything* because I think it's important for you to feel what you need to feel. But I will promise you that no matter what happens, I'll be there. There's nothing you can do that will force me away, Poppy. You're not a bad person; you just got caught up with a bad man. That's all over now. You can take a deep breath and relax knowing that he can never hurt you again. No one can, because I won't allow it. You're safe, and it's okay to move forward and leave this behind you. I'm not saying *not* to feel what you're feeling, I'm just saying that I'm here to help you see the positive side of things."

"I don't know what I did to deserve a friend like you," she whispered, leaning in to hug me.

Even though we were technically *friends*, I couldn't help but feel the pain of the dagger that pierced my heart when she said it.

****

A few hours later, we were cooking dinner together in the kitchen while she hummed Christmas songs under her breath. I hated that it was only a few weeks until Christmas, and I didn't have a single decoration up. She was stuck with me while trying to deal with everything with her husband, so the least I could do was make her stay here a little more festive.

I set the ladle down and jogged into the living room, laughing when Travis went with me. He didn't stop and smacked right into the couch, leaving him a little dazed as he looked up at me with those sad puppy eyes.

"You have to be careful, buddy," I said as I picked up the chewed-up TV remote and scratched the top of his head. "You're not as big or tough as you think you are."

He whined and laid down, showing me his belly.

"Not right now," I told him, shaking my head. "I'll give you tummy scratches later. Right now I have to make dinner."

He continued laying there, not giving a damn what I had to say. I pulled up my music app and found a Christmas playlist, making sure it was loud enough for Poppy to hear. Her head perked up when she heard the song she had been humming start to play.

I set the remote out of Travis's reach and went back to the kitchen, returning Poppy's smile as I opened the oven and checked on the meatloaf.

It had been a long time since I'd made meatloaf, but I wanted to make a comforting meal for her tonight. Even though we knew why she had killed Dale, it didn't erase the feelings that had threatened to consume her that she had taken a life. Just because she didn't love him and needed to protect herself didn't mean she was void of emotion.

I pulled the meatloaf out of the oven and set it on the trivet before stirring the gravy. Poppy had insisted on mashing the potatoes, and I didn't fight her on it when I saw how much force she was using. She needed to burn off some energy, and I got it. I wasn't going to stand in the way of her giving those potatoes hell.

Once dinner was ready, I pulled two plates out and handed her one, waiting for her to serve herself.

"You go first," she said, stepping away from the counter and clutching the plate against her chest.

I shook my head and frowned.

"I don't think so. Ladies first," I replied, extending my hand as I did some weird bowing motion that she giggled at.

"Please, Pat. Just get your food."

I took a deep breath and then let it out slowly, not wanting to pick a fight with her.

I stepped in front of her and began scooping some of the meatloaf out of the pan and setting it on the plate. Then I added some mashed potatoes and started to pour gravy, but stopped.

"Are you one of those people who like gravy on your meatloaf, or am I just weird?" I asked, looking at her over my shoulder.

"No," she replied with a laugh. "I like it too. It makes the meatloaf taste better if it's soaked in gravy."

I nodded my head and grinned as I drenched the meatloaf and mashed potatoes in gravy. Once it looked like a decent-sized serving, I spun around and extended the plate to Poppy.

"What are you doing?" she asked with a nervous laugh.

"Serving you." I raised my eyebrows at the plate in my hand and nodded for her to take it.

"Patrick Ray Hughes! That's cheating!" Her beautiful blue eyes lit up as she tried not to laugh.

"You just middle named me," I replied, clutching a hand to my chest as if she had wounded me as she took the plate and passed me the one she had been holding.

"You deserve it. That was a sneaky move."

"Well, I wanted you to go first, but you refused. So, I had to improvise."

"I shall remember this and get you back," she teased as she

set her plate down on the kitchen table and pulled out the chair.

I couldn't remember the last time I'd eaten at the table and not on the couch, but it seemed to be the thing Poppy and I did. It was really nice to sit down and focus on the conversation we were having, instead of relying on the TV for company. On rare occasions, my parents would come over, but most of the time, I would go to their condo. Aside from my niece, Daisy, no one else visited that often. I used to think I liked my solitude, but Poppy was making me question everything I thought I knew and wanted.

"Oh my God, this meatloaf is incredible," Poppy said around a mouthful of food as she held her hand in front of her mouth and chewed.

"Thank you. I'm glad you like it."

I lifted my fork and took a bite, nearly choking when Poppy closed her eyes and softly moaned as she chewed another bite.

Fuck. We hadn't had sex since the first time the other day, but I had somehow managed to force the sounds out of my head in an effort to preserve my sanity as I tried to maintain a proper boundary with her. Hearing it now had my dick straining against my jeans as I remembered just how good she sounded when she loved something. I had done my best to stay away from Poppy so that my desire for her wouldn't cloud my judgment when it came to keeping her safe, but this was pushing it.

I took a sip of water, hoping to wash down the food before Poppy realized my life was literally on the line because of her moaning.

When she opened her eyes and saw the look I was giving her, she blushed and nervously tucked a strand of hair behind her ear.

"Sorry. I umm… I sometimes get a little vocal when I'm enjoying something."

"I remember," I said softly, letting the weight of my words sit between us as I clenched my fork tightly so I didn't do anything stupid, like lunge across the table and devour her.

"You know Gage is stupid, right?" she asked, setting her fork down as she leveled me with a look.

"Why do you say that?"

"Because he is. While I love him dearly because he's my cousin, I think he's stupid if he thinks he can stop whatever this is between us from happening."

"It's not just Gage," I said, exhaling heavily. "My focus needs to be on you and helping you through whatever happens with the whole Dale thing. I can't do that if I'm constantly fucking you—because we both know that we would be going at it nonstop if given the opportunity."

"I know."

"Just because they found his body and you filed a police report doesn't mean that you're in the clear. We still have to wait for the autopsy report. If they find anything suspicious, you could still become their primary suspect. Anything is possible, and I can't risk getting distracted and letting something bad happen to you."

"I get that. I do. But hear me out," she said softly. "What about quickies? I mean, technically, there is no danger that we need to be worried about. Dale is dead, so it's not like he can come back and try to kill me or get revenge. We've already spoken with the police, and I've filed a report. I don't see what else can go wrong. Even if the autopsy shows foul play, they would have to be able to prove that I killed him and dragged him out of the house, into the garage, then loaded him into the car. There's a lot they would have to dig through, and I don't know if it's even possible to still detect it, but his blood alcohol level would have been incredibly high given the amount of whiskey he had that night. Who's to say he didn't fall and hurt himself before driving drunk and crashing the car before ending up in the river?"

She grinned so hard at me that it was almost impossible not to smile back at her.

"See, nothing to worry about," she pressed as she took another bite.

"I don't think that's how any of this works," I countered. "The last thing I want is for law enforcement to show up here and arrest you because they think you killed him. Not only that, we still have to worry about the FBI and the account he has that now goes to you. There's a lot at play here, Poppy. We can't afford to make mistakes because we're horny."

"You take all of the fun out of this." She pretended to glare at me as she lifted her fork and resumed eating.

"Believe me, this isn't fun for me either. I would rather have *you* spread out on this table and eating your sweet pussy instead of this fucking meatloaf," I groaned, stabbing at it with my fork.

"Too bad Travis isn't a guard dog. He could buy us some time."

"He'd probably lick them to death if anyone tried to come into the cabin. He's the worst guard dog I've ever seen. We've put him with Gage's dog, Duke, hoping that he could teach Travis a thing or two, but even Duke gets irritated with him." I laughed as I looked over at Travis, who was chewing on one of the wooden legs of the couch.

Fucking dog.

"Eh, it's probably for the best," Poppy said as she leaned back and pushed her plate forward.

"Why's that?"

"Because I've been thinking about this trick I learned a while back, where I hum while I suck your cock, and I thought I could try it on you. But maybe it's better that we don't do that. I wouldn't want you to get obsessed with my mind-blowing oral skills."

She got up and took her plate to the counter, her fingers brushing over my shoulder as she walked past.

"Too fucking late for that," I muttered, finishing my food that no longer tasted good.

Nothing would ever taste as good as Poppy.

82

Sixteen
Poppy

Patrick had gotten up before me, but I could still smell the fresh scent of his body wash as it floated out of the bathroom. I hated how much I enjoyed the smell of it, mainly because it reminded me of the time I watched him jack off in the shower before we had the most mind-blowing sex. While I understood why he said we couldn't keep messing around, it didn't mean that I liked it.

It had been four days since we'd received a visit from the Silver Falls police and I'd filed a report. It felt oddly liberating to document the abuse I'd suffered at the hands of my husband, even though nothing could be done about it now. At the end of the day, I was at peace knowing that he could never hurt me or anyone else ever again.

I'd gotten a call from the funeral home after the morgue released the body to them, asking what I wanted to do with his body. It was hard to decide because I didn't care what happened; I just wanted all of this to be over. The cost of the autopsy was covered by the Silver Falls Police Department, since they requested it. But the cost of transporting him back to Coyote Creek and burying him would fall on me since I was legally the next of kin. Given that I wasn't currently working, I didn't have a ton of disposable income to deal with this.

Patrick had suggested that I contact the Coyote Creek Sheriff's Department to see if they would cover the expense to bring one of their own home, which they happily did. I explained to the funeral home that Detective Gomez would be handling the arrangements and that they should contact him for any additional information. While I still had to go to the funeral home and sign paperwork, at least I didn't have to look at his body. It was offered, but I quickly refused and had a mild panic attack, which Patrick played off as grief so they didn't question what was wrong with me.

I knew that I would have to go back to Coyote Creek in a few days to deal with his body once it got there, but for now, I just wanted to focus on today. I took a shower and then went in search of Patrick as I heard Christmas music playing in the kitchen.

When I walked in, Patrick was standing on a ladder, attempting to hang a strand of Christmas lights above the large window in the living room. His shirt lifted as he reached higher, giving me an unobstructed view of his abs in the process.

I cleared my throat to let him know I was there, so I wouldn't startle him and cause him to fall off the ladder.

"Good morning," he said, glancing down at me before returning his focus to the lights. He pulled them tighter, securing them on a nail sticking out of the wall before letting the rest of the strand fall as he climbed down the ladder.

"Good morning. I see you've been busy this morning," I commented, grinning when I noticed all of the Christmas decorations he'd put up. I looked up, noticing the mistletoe hanging right above us.

"That I have. I needed something to take my mind off of fucking you, so I decided to put holes in the wall and hang some shit." He shoved his hands in his pockets as he rocked back on his heels before leaning in to brush a light kiss across my lips. My heart fluttered as heat spread through me.

"I'm sorry—" I paused to laugh, his words catching up in my brain. "You needed something to take your mind off of *what*?"

"Fucking you," he clarified as he stood in front of me and his eyes locked on mine. "You were laying on your stomach, and when you kicked the sheets off, I got a perfect view of your ass. And since you decided to forgo panties last night, I also got to see your pussy."

"Oh." I pressed my lips together to keep from laughing. Yep, I had done that on purpose, hoping he would get a good look at what we both knew he wanted.

"Don't try to act like you didn't do that shit on purpose," he said, pointing his finger at me. "You're a sneaky little minx, but I'm onto you."

"Well, I wish you were inside of me, but on *top* of me works too." I grinned widely as he pretended to be frustrated with me.

"You're going to be the death of me. You do know that, right?"

"You wouldn't be my first," I teased, but the energy in the room immediately shifted with the truth in my words. I shook my head and looked down at the floor, too embarrassed to look at him.

"Help me decorate the tree," Patrick said, pinching the bottom of my chin to force my gaze up to his.

"You can't just demand that I do stuff," I countered, narrowing my eyes.

"Okay. Help me decorate the tree, *please*."

"Better." I nodded my head in approval and giggled as he shook his head and reached for me.

I knew that he meant it to be playful, but something about the way his hand tried to grab mine made me step back and freeze. We both realized what had happened before either of us could say anything.

"I'm so sorry, Poppy," he apologized quickly.

"No—" I said, holding up my hand to stop him. "I shouldn't be like this, for fucks sake. It's frustrating. I know you're not trying to hurt me."

He kept his distance but didn't take his eyes off me.

"While I would never try to hurt you, that doesn't erase the fact that he *did* hurt you. These reactions are valid, Poppy. You can't expect them to just stop because he's no longer here. You spent six months having to live through this; your body is conditioned to react in a way that protects you from his harm. That's okay. I'm sorry for what I did. I should have thought about it before I reached for you."

"I want you to be able to do those things, Pat. I want to be able to lean into your touch without punching you or freaking out."

"Time, Poppy. It's going to take time. You can't just turn off what happened to you and expect everything to be okay because he's dead. You have to heal first. You have to let yourself feel all of the things you never allowed yourself to feel when you were with him. You're safe now, so it's okay to fall apart."

"I don't want to fall apart," I objected. "I want to keep my shit together and be around someone who I genuinely like without worrying about how my stupid body is going to react when he tries to touch me."

Patrick grinned and took a small step closer to me, slowly extending his hands until I took them.

"Like I said, it's okay to fall apart. Tacos fall apart, and I still love them."

"Yeah, but that's because you eat tacos…"

I stopped and chewed the side of my lip as I watched his eyes darken with what I said.

"Do you want me to eat you like a taco, Poppy?" he asked, taking another step closer until his chest nearly brushed against mine. "Do you want to fall apart in my mouth as I eat you?"

I nodded, too aroused to say anything.

Patrick's grin somehow got bigger and took on a mischievous edge before he leaned forward and whispered in my ear.

"I'm about to turn into a total fucking caveman and carry you over my shoulder all the way up to my bed so I can devour you the way I want to. You good with that?"

I squealed and nodded as a wave of excitement rushed through me.

<u>Seventeen</u>
Patrick

I laid on my stomach as I slid my tongue between Poppy's lips, loving the way her arousal tasted. Her skin was still soft from her shower and smelled like the body wash I loved on her. While I knew that we shouldn't be doing this, there was nothing that was going to stop me at this point.

Her fingers dug into my hair, gripping it tightly as I sucked her clit. She was close to coming, even though I hadn't been down there long. It seemed she was as wound up and frustrated as I was, both of us desperately needing a release.

A few more flicks of my tongue and some strong sucking, and I felt her spasm around my face as she cried out and pulled my hair. Watching Poppy come undone was one of the most beautiful things I'd ever seen. But *feeling* her come undone at my touch was pure heaven.

I slid up her naked body, taking my time as her eyes fluttered open and she smiled at me. Her hand reached for my cock, but I moved out of the way because there was no way I was ready for any of this to be over this quickly. And letting her touch my dick right now was a surefire way to get me there in record time.

I hovered over her, not wanting to smash her under the weight of my body as I gently nudged her head to the side with mine before trailing kisses down her neck. She shuddered beneath me as goosebumps spread over her skin. I could feel the warmth of her pussy against my stomach as my cock strained with arousal. It would be so easy to just slide inside of her right now and fuck her the way I wanted to fuck her.

"Do it," she whispered, as if somehow reading my mind. "Put us both out of our misery and fuck me already."

I chuckled and shook my head as I pulled back and studied her. She was, by far, the most beautiful woman I'd ever seen in my life.

"I need to grab a condom," I said, pulling away to get one from the nightstand.

"Hurry. I'm practically dying over here."

"You're being a bit dramatic," I teased, grabbing one and sheathing myself quickly. "You just came like two minutes ago."

"Yes, but coming is *not* the same as having a hard cock inside of me. There's a *big* difference, my friend, and right now, you're withholding the cock."

"My apologies. I won't let it happen again."

I resumed my position and braced myself on my forearm as I lined my cock up at her entrance and slowly pushed inside. Her eyes closed as she let out a soft hiss before her body started to relax around me. It seemed impossible, but somehow I had already forgotten how tight her pussy was and had to grip the sheets to keep from blowing my load as it gripped me tightly.

"Fuck," I moaned, pausing for a second to get a hold of myself.

"Nope. Not happening," she scolded quickly as she dug her nails into my ass. "You're not going to give me the cock just to turn around and not *give* me the cock."

"I'm trying not to come right away," I explained as I looked down at her beautiful blue eyes staring up at me.

"I don't care if you come right away. I. Want. You. To. Fuck. Me. Right. Now. Hard. Fast. I want it all, so if you can't get this party started, roll over and I will."

"Man, you're really bossy when you're horny," I teased.

"Trust me, you don't want to see the lengths I will go to—"

She stopped and gasped as I pulled out and slammed inside of her, grinning when I felt her back arch as her legs fell open to allow me in.

"What were you saying?" I asked, pushing her legs up until they were tucked into her chest, and her pussy was on full display. I looked down and watched as I pulled out, my cock glistening with her arousal on the condom, before I slowly pushed inside, watching it disappear.

Before she could answer, I pulled out and slammed into her, repeating the motion as my thrusts got harder and faster.

She closed her eyes and enjoyed the ride while I fucked her the way we both needed to be fucked right now. Her body was so responsive to me that it didn't surprise me when I rubbed her clit with my thumb and brought her to orgasm again in just a few seconds. Constantly feeling her body react to my touch was the positive reassurance I didn't know I needed in life. It was as if I didn't have any choice but to live to bring her pleasure.

My balls tightened as I increased my pace, sending myself over the edge as I released into the condom, wishing it were her pussy instead.

A warmth spread through me as she opened her eyes and gazed at me with a look of pure satisfaction and contentment on her face.

It was at that moment that I realized the truth of what had happened.

I hadn't just fucked Poppy.

I'd fallen in love with her.

Eighteen
Poppy

I hadn't just had sex with Patrick—he'd fucked me senseless. Or at least that was what I used as my excuse when I looked down at my phone and found a handful of new text messages, though I hadn't heard an alert for them.

I opened my phone and frowned at the unknown number, wondering what kind of solicitation it was this time. I had suspected it was about them trying to reach me to discuss my extended car warranty, but my stomach soured when I read the first one.

UNKNOWN: I know what you did.

UNKNOWN: Did you really think you'd get away with it?

UNKNOWN: You should know by now that there are cameras everywhere.

UNKNOWN: Here's a secret: Dale wasn't who you thought he was, and neither am I.

UNKNOWN: I'll be waiting.

I covered my mouth and stared at the screen, processing

each message as my hand trembled. Patrick had gone downstairs to let Travis out while I cleaned up, but I hadn't heard him come back. When he suddenly appeared in the bedroom, I gasped and dropped the phone.

"Poppy? What's wrong?" he asked, his brows furrowing in concern.

I shook my head and looked around the room as if that would somehow tell me who had sent those text messages.

"Poppy, you're starting to freak me out. What happened?"

My lip trembled as I tried to gather the strength I needed to tell him.

"Someone knows that I killed Dale."

Nineteen
Patrick

"I understand, but isn't there some other way to track the number?" I asked, shoving my hand through my hair as I held the phone to my ear.

I had been on the phone with my friend, Keith, for the last ten minutes while Gage and Julie sat in the kitchen, talking to Poppy. I had called Gage as soon as I found out about the text messages, and they came over right away. My niece, Daisy, was out shopping with my parents but would be back in a few hours, so I wanted to get as much done as possible while she was away. The last thing I needed was to traumatize her after everything she'd already been through.

Keith confirmed that there was nothing they could do to figure out who the text messages came from, but that he would be happy to help if anything came up. While I trusted him more than most people, I also hated the uncomfortable feeling I held deep down about talking to him about anything related to Poppy, given that he worked for the FBI and her dead husband was being investigated by them.

I hung up and set my phone on the coffee table, taking a few deep breaths before heading to join the others in the kitchen. It felt like I was living another nightmare after what happened last year with my sister. I knew the situation was different, but I couldn't help but feel a little like John McClane from the Die Hard movies because having a calm, peaceful Christmas seemed impossible. Between my sister's obsessed stalker last year and Poppy's dead husband this year, I was a little terrified to celebrate the holiday next year.

"What did Keith say?" Gage asked, standing behind the couch with his arms folded over his chest.

"Exactly what we thought he would. There's no way to trace the number to anyone, given it's a burner phone."

He nodded and worked his jaw back and forth.

"It's going to be okay," he said, catching me off guard.

"I know."

I swallowed hard, forcing the negative thoughts away because I didn't have time to worry about the worst-case scenario right now. My only concern at the moment was the woman sitting at my kitchen table, crying as my sister held her. While it was concerning the messages she received, I would die before I allowed anything to happen to Poppy.

The tension between Gage and me wasn't as bad when they showed up earlier, but I didn't know if it was because he had gotten over being mad or if it was because there was an actual problem to deal with now. Either way, I was thankful that he seemed relatively calm about Poppy and me.

I got off the couch and walked into the kitchen behind Gage as Julie pulled away from Poppy and handed her some tissues. Poppy got up, and when she turned to face me, she stopped.

It was hard to read the look on her face because it was a mix of worry and sadness combined.

I opened my arms and let out a sigh of relief as she fell into them, allowing me to hold her the way I needed to. I closed my eyes and let my chest fall as I exhaled heavily, breathing her scent in with my next breath. This was where I wanted to spend the rest of my life, with this woman who had changed me so much in such a short time.

I felt Gage's eyes on us, but ignored him. Just because Poppy and I had sex didn't mean anything had officially changed between us. We were still technically just friends who were fucking. While I wanted more, I would never ask her for anything right now, given what she was going through.

But that didn't stop the yearning I felt deep inside. Poppy wasn't mine to protect, but I would stop at nothing to keep the woman I was falling in love with safe. No matter how much my best friend had to say about it.

98

Twenty
Poppy

I sat and stared at my phone for an enormous amount of time, waiting for more text messages that never came. Finally, Patrick said it was enough and forced me to leave the house. We went into town to grab a few things from the store before another big storm rolled through, but I was more surprised when he pulled into the parking lot of the local steakhouse and parked.

"What are you doing?" I asked, looking around as he studied my face.

"I'm taking you on a date," he replied, swallowing hard and trying to smile, though I could tell his nerves were getting the better of him.

"A date?" My eyebrows rose almost as high as my voice before it cracked.

"Yes. A date." He cleared his throat and looked around for a few seconds before he looked at me. "I know that you have a lot going on right now, and I'm not trying to make anything harder for you. I promise. But I can't lie and say that I haven't developed feelings for you, Poppy. So, yes, I would like it if you'd allow me the honor of taking you on a date tonight."

I licked my lips and shifted in my seat so I could see him better. He was so freaking handsome.

"I have feelings for you, too," I admitted, noticing the way my heart raced when I said it. "A lot of feelings." I giggled, the whole idea of us doing this reminding me of high school kids admitting they have a crush on each other.

"I hope they're good feelings," he teased, raising an eyebrow.

"They're the best."

"So, I can take you on a date?"

I laughed at the tone of his voice and how uncertain he still seemed, even though I had just confirmed I liked him too.

"Yes, you can take me on a date. But I have to warn you, I don't put out on the first date."

He shook his head as he got out of the truck and rushed around to open my door for me. He extended his hand and helped me, making sure I didn't slip on the slush beneath me.

"Do any of the previous meals that we've shared by chance count as dates?" he asked as I slid my arm into his and walked alongside him the short distance to the door of the steakhouse.

"Yeah, I guess we can count those." I scrunched my nose and then laughed again when he jerked his arm in a *yes* motion.

We walked inside, and I was surprised by how fancy it

was, given how small Silver Falls was. I was used to seeing them in bigger cities, but hadn't ever seen one in the small towns I visited.

The room was dimly lit, with soft music playing over the speakers, as we followed the hostess to a booth in the back. I took my seat and pulled the napkin from the plate, setting it in my lap as Patrick sat across from me and did the same. Within a few seconds, a man approached the table, pouring fresh ice water into our glasses while another young kid delivered a basket of bread and some dipping oils.

"Wow," I said after they left. "This is quite the service already."

"It's one of my favorite restaurants in Silver Falls," Patrick said, smiling softly. "It reminds me of New York."

"Do you miss living in the big city?"

"Sometimes." He shrugged and let his shoulders fall. "I enjoy being close to family more."

"I can see that. Daisy is such an amazing little girl, and her face lights up the second she sees you. I know your mother hasn't stopped talking about how happy she is that her family is all in the same town again, and your dad, well…"

"He's my dad," Patrick replied with a laugh. "Always easy going and happy in general. But you should see him with Daisy. I thought *I* was her favorite, but when my dad is around, it's like I don't even exist."

"I'm happy she has you guys. I love that for her."

I looked off into the distance, forcing the thoughts of my childhood away from the surface. This was a nice night out with Patrick, and I didn't want to taint it by thinking about how I longed to feel loved as a child and never did.

Just then, a woman appeared at our table wearing a crisp white button-down shirt and black dress pants.

"Hello, welcome to Rufigio's. I'm Belle, and I'll be taking care of you tonight. May I start you with some wine or perhaps a signature cocktail from the bar?"

I had no idea whether Patrick drank wine because he hadn't drunk anything but water and coffee in the time I'd been staying with him.

"I'll have an Old Fashioned, please," Patrick said, looking at me instead of the waitress.

"I'll have a Dirty Martini, please," I replied, smiling at the waitress as she nodded and headed to the bar to place our order.

I knew she would be back shortly with the drinks and ready to take our order, so I picked up the menu and looked it over. There were only a few options, but they all looked delicious, so it was hard to choose.

"What do you get here?" I asked Patrick, glancing at him over the top of the menu.

"I like the ribeye with the roasted garlic mashed potatoes," he replied, looking at his.

I nodded and looked over the menu again, debating whether to get what he was getting or to be more ladylike and order a smaller cut of meat instead. Before I could decide, the waitress appeared, setting our drinks on the table.

"Would you like a few more minutes to look over the

menu?" she asked, clasping her hands in front of her.

I felt Patrick's eyes on me as he waited to answer.

"I think I'll do the ribeye with the roasted garlic mashed potatoes," I answered, fighting a giggle when I saw the corners of his lips curl up into a smile.

I set the menu down on the table and looked at him, loving how incredibly sexy he was. He had a laid-back charisma about him, but what was even more attractive was how he acknowledged the waitress and treated her with respect, all while looking at me like he wanted to spread me across the table and eat me. It was a fine line that he seemed to have mastered perfectly.

"I'll do the same," he said, collecting both of our menus and handing them to the waitress.

"Perfect. I'll put this in now. Would you like any appetizers to start with?" She looked between us, but the heat I felt from his gaze had me shaking my head no instead of verbally answering her.

She smiled, bowed her head, and walked off, leaving us alone.

"This is a really nice place," I said as I reached across the table and wrapped my fingers in his.

He lifted our hands and brushed a kiss against my knuckles, sending a shiver through me.

"I'm glad you like it."

We stayed staring at each other for a few seconds before I looked away, desperate for some relief from the ache that was building between my thighs from the thoughts of what I knew he could do to my body.

Patrick leaned against the plush leather of the booth and adjusted himself under the table while I took a sip of my martini. It had been a long time since I'd had a drink, mainly because I didn't trust myself to be even slightly inebriated around Dale. After getting drunk and married in Las Vegas, I stopped drinking immediately after that.

But the difference now was that I felt safe with Patrick, which let me lower my walls and let him in. It had been so long since I'd felt even slightly this comfortable with someone that I was still a little nervous to let him *all the way* in.

Soon, our dinner arrived, and we made idle conversation about Christmas and what gifts he wanted to get for Daisy while we ate. The food was incredible, but the company was better than anything I'd ever experienced. While Patrick limited himself to one drink because he was driving, I decided to allow myself a little freedom and had a second martini while we finished dinner.

I had been so caught up in our conversation that I hadn't noticed the man sitting across the room at another table, staring at me, until Patrick had gone to the restroom. A glass of water sat in front of him beside a basket of bread that didn't appear to be touched. There was something about him, the way he was looking at me, that sent a shiver through me and made my blood turn to ice.

I tried to get a better look at him, but it was too dark to see him from so far away. The sound of blood rushing through my ears kept me from hearing Patrick as he returned, startling me as my eyes shot up to him as he slid into the booth and then froze.

I looked from him back to the table where the man had been sitting, my stomach dropping when it was suddenly empty.

"What's wrong?" Patrick asked, leaning forward as he turned to look past the tall wall that divided our booth from the one behind him.

"There was… there… a man… I…" I pressed my lips together and shook my head. I needed to get it together and stop letting fear overcome me. "There was a man sitting in that booth, and he was watching me."

"Where?"

I pointed to where he had been sitting, the full glass of ice water and bread on the table untouched.

"What did he look like?"

"I don't know," I said with a shrug, trying to remember as much as I could. "It was really hard to see anything with the dim lights and how far away he was. He seemed thin, but I couldn't tell you anything else."

"Did you see what he was wearing?"

I shook my head, trying to remember as Patrick got up from the booth and waited.

"I think maybe a solid, dark colored button-down shirt and jeans. I don't know, Pat. It was hard to see anything."

Before I could say anything else, he sprinted off, nearly knocking a server over on his way.

I leaned back in the booth and tried to regulate my breathing as our waitress approached, concern on her face as she looked from me to the direction Patrick had run off.

"Is everything okay?" she asked, standing beside the table.

"Yeah. Just a little mix-up," I lied, forcing a smile.

"I'll leave this here for when you guys are ready. No rush," she replied as she set the check down on Patrick's side of the table.

Shit. She probably thought he was trying to run out on paying the bill.

I grabbed my purse, pulled out my wallet, and took out a credit card just as Patrick returned. His face was red from the cold, and he was slightly out of breath.

"Are you okay?" I asked, reaching for the check holder on the table.

He sat down and grabbed it before I could, and pulled out his wallet.

"I'm fine. Are you okay?"

I nodded, extending my credit card to him.

"I don't think so," he replied, smiling as the waitress returned and took it from him after he slid his credit card inside. "I didn't bring you to dinner to have you pay for it."

"I seriously don't care about that," I insisted. "I'm happy to pay."

"And I would hate for you to pay on our date, Poppy. I wanted to take you out and have a nice dinner together, my treat."

"Did you find the guy?"

He shook his head no and then smiled again as the waitress

returned and set the check holder down beside him so he could sign the receipt.

"I was asked to give this to you," the waitress said, handing me a folded-up piece of paper.

My eyes widened as Patrick's brows furrowed. I reached out a shaky hand and took it, waiting to open it until she left.

"Do you know the person who gave it to you?" Patrick asked her.

"No, unfortunately, it was given to the hostess who asked if I could deliver it since she had a new party that needed to be seated. I didn't see the person who left it with her."

"Thank you," Patrick said, dismissing her.

"Thank you for joining us tonight. I hope you have a wonderful evening." She gave both of us a smile and walked off to greet her new table.

"What does it say?" Patrick asked, his body as tense as mine was.

My fingers trembled as I unfolded it and stared at the neat black ink on the paper.

"Found you," I said, my lips quivering as I tossed the paper down and stared at it.

"We need to go. Now." Patrick's energy changed as he got up and looked at the note on the table. He went to reach for it when I held my hand out and stopped him.

"It could have fingerprints on it," I explained, stopping for a second before I opened my purse and pulled out a tissue from the pocket-sized pack I kept in there. I grabbed the end of the note with the tissue, then folded it around it, hoping I didn't wipe off any fingerprints. It wasn't like we had any other options and I wasn't willing to wait around for law enforcement to show up, just because I got a creepy note.

I tucked it into my purse, then zipped it shut and accepted his hand as he helped me out of the booth. My legs were shaky as we made our way outside, his hand protectively on my lower back the entire time. We got in the truck, and I barely had time to get my seatbelt buckled before he was putting it in drive and getting us the hell out of there.

Twenty-One
Patrick

The truck slipped on the ice-covered road back to the cabin as I pushed through the snow that was falling around us, going faster than I should. Knowing that someone had been there and left a creepy note for Poppy at the steakhouse had left me desperate to get her back to the cabin, where I knew she would be safe.

My hands gripped the steering wheel tightly as I tried to focus on the road and not the racing thoughts flooding my brain about what had happened. I had rushed out of the restaurant as quickly as possible, hopeful I would catch the asshole. By the time I got outside, the parking lot was eerily silent with no one coming or going.

I let out a heavy breath as the cabin came into view and paused for a second while I considered whether we should stop by the inn to fill Gage and Julie in. While it would be great to have safety in numbers, I couldn't willingly take Poppy there and risk something happening that would put Daisy in danger.

By the time I parked in front of the cabin, I couldn't shake the feeling that something was wrong. I parked and got out to help Poppy, but the hairs standing up on my arms made me stop.

"What's wrong?" she asked, pulling her coat tighter around her body as she scanned my face while I searched the woods around us. It was dark out, and aside from the lights we left on in the cabin, I couldn't see anything.

Then it hit me.

The lights we had left on.

"Get back in the truck," I said urgently, pushing her back toward it as I listened for any signs of danger.

"Pat—"

"Now," I warned, pinning her with a look that made her nod and climb back inside.

I hated that I didn't have a weapon on me and that we were alone in the middle of the woods. Either the storm had knocked the power out, or someone had been in my cabin.

I grabbed my phone and pulled it out, taking soft steps as I looked around. Thankfully, my eyes had already adjusted to the darkness, so I could see if there was any movement in the trees. I glanced at Poppy, making sure she was safe in the truck as it rang against my ear.

"What's up?" Gage answered.

"Did the power go out?"

"No, not here anyway. Why? Is it out at your place?"

"Yeah."

"How long has it been out?"

"I don't know. We just got back from dinner. Someone was at the restaurant watching Poppy and left a creepy note for her after they left. Now we're home, and I know I left the lights on before we left, but now—"

"I'm on my way."

The line went dead as he hung up, so I put the phone back in my pocket and walked around to the side of the cabin. It was a quiet night as the snow fell around me, making it impossible to see if there were any footprints.

The sound of Gage's truck caught my attention, but I didn't pull my focus away from the cabin as I heard him get out and walk over.

"Where's Poppy?" he asked, standing beside me as we stared at the front door.

"In the truck."

"Have you been inside yet?"

"Nope."

"Go ahead. I've got you covered out here," he said.

He didn't have to say any more for me to read between the lines and know what he meant.

I walked to the front door and examined the door handle, noticing some of the wood was splintered.

"Someone's been inside," I said over my shoulder.

While I knew that whoever had broken in might still be there and hear me talking, I would rather that he be aware of the threat so he could take action if needed.

I pushed the door open, listening for the distinct sound of pitter-patter from Travis, and frowned when I didn't hear it. He didn't so much as even whine, which was unusual. I reached my hand along the wall and found the light switch, flipping it up as the lights turned on.

I walked slowly, looking into the kitchen before finding Travis lying on the floor. I knelt down, immediately looking for a sign that he was still alive when he whimpered. They'd done something to him, but I didn't know what. I didn't have time to check on him because I didn't know if they were still in the house.

Quietly, I stepped over him and grabbed a knife from the block on the counter, and held it at my side as I worked quickly to clear the kitchen and living room. I checked every nook and cranny to make sure no one was hiding before I went upstairs.

The guest room was still as I had left it, and nothing had been tampered with in the bathrooms as far as I could tell.

But I stopped in my tracks as I stood in front of the bed and stared at the photos scattered across it. In the middle was a piece of paper with the word "murderer" written in black marker.

Twenty-Two
Poppy

I covered my mouth to keep from screaming while my stomach threatened to dispel the dinner we'd just finished not that long ago. I stared at the pictures on the bed and trembled as Patrick kept his hand wrapped around my waist while he spoke to a Silver Falls police officer.

Gage stayed by the bedroom door, keeping an eye on things, just in case the intruder decided to come back. They'd both searched the house top to bottom, but hadn't found anyone.

Most of the pictures were of me in Las Vegas the night I married Dale. I had no idea who had taken them because it was just us, and I was drunk. I hadn't paid attention to who was around us and thought I was having the time of my life. A few of the photos were of me in the ICU in Coyote Creek, which was even more disturbing because I hadn't had any visitors that I could recall. What was even more alarming were the ones next to the note that said *murderer,* because those were taken inside Patrick's cabin.

"Fucking hell," Patrick growled, pulling away slightly to put his cell phone in his pocket.

"What did they say?" Gage asked as I stood there, continuing to stare at the bed.

"They can't send anyone out because of the storm. We'll have to wait until it passes and they can get someone out here."

"So what are you supposed to do with all of that?" Gage pointed to the items on the bed.

"They said to try to collect what I can and put it in a Ziplock bag. I'm supposed to wear gloves to avoid getting any new fingerprints on them, but my guess is whoever did this was smart enough not to leave any behind in the first place."

"I'll go grab some bags," Gage said before turning and leaving us alone.

"It's going to be okay," Patrick said, letting out a frustrated sigh as he gently rubbed a hand down my back.

"I should have left," I replied, refusing to look at him as I stared at the images that would haunt me forever.

"What do you mean?"

"When I first got here. I should have left after I came to see Gage. I should have gone back to Coyote Creek, where I belong."

Patrick moved, stepping in front of me as he blocked my view. Very slowly, he raised his hand and brushed his fingers gently against my cheek.

"This is where you belong," he said softly. "Here with me."

I shook my head, wanting to pull away from his touch

because I didn't deserve his love or affection right now. Because of me, someone had broken into his cabin and hurt his dog. I couldn't live with myself if anything happened to those I was quickly starting to love because of me.

Gage returned a few seconds later, wearing a pair of nitrile gloves he found with the cleaning supplies. He picked up each photo by the corner, tossed it into the Ziplock bag, and then added the piece of paper with the note on it.

I grabbed my purse, pulled out the tissue that had the note from the restaurant, and slipped it inside with the other stuff.

"I'll take this to the inn and keep it safe until the police can collect it," Gage said. "You guys can come stay with us tonight. The upstairs is still being remodeled, but you can stay in one of the rooms downstairs."

"Thank you, but no," I said, pulling my shoulders back and standing straight as I faced my cousin.

"Why not?"

"Because I have already brought enough trouble with me as it is. I'm not going to let something happen to you guys because I got myself into a bad situation. I appreciate the offer, but no. Patrick is more than welcome to go—"

"Like fuck I am," he growled, his anger matching the frustration etched on his face. "I'm not leaving your side, Poppy. Better get those thoughts out of your head now, because I'm not going anywhere."

"I don't think it's a good idea for you guys to stay here," Gage said, his tone even for once instead of angry. "Someone has already been inside your cabin. What makes you think they won't come back?"

"I know. Trust me, I don't like it either. But the roads are only going to get worse with that storm, so it's not like we can head into town and get a hotel," Patrick replied with a heavy exhale. "I agree with Poppy, I'm not comfortable staying at the inn and putting Julie and Daisy at risk either."

"Then I guess that means we either stay here, or we sleep in your truck," I offered, my attention on Patrick and not on my cousin as he clenched his jaw and shook his head.

"I'll secure the cabin," he said, turning to face Gage. "I have some scraps of wood I can use for the door, and I'll move the furniture in the living room to block the back door and windows. If anyone tries to get in, I'll hear them."

"Do you have protection?" Gage asked, his hand moving toward the back of his jeans.

"I'm good. I have two that are fully loaded and plenty of ammunition."

"Poppy has a good aim, don't be afraid to let her help," Gage said, nodding at me.

My heart fluttered with warmth at what my cousin had said. We'd spent a lot of time growing up outside shooting soda cans and making up targets, but I was surprised he remembered that I had been good at it. While I hadn't shot anything in a long time, it had always been like second nature to me, and guns never made me uneasy. It was like I was born to know how to handle one.

"Absolutely. I'll make sure we both have what we need," Patrick agreed.

"Call if you need anything. I can be here in four minutes, tops. I'll bring Duke over. He'll alert you if anyone comes near the cabin."

"Thanks, Gage," I said softly, offering him the best smile I could manage. "I think we'll be just fine. Keep Duke there so we know that Daisy is protected. I know how much he means to her."

"She'll be fine," Gage started, but stopped when Patrick shot him a look. "Alright. Well, if you change your mind, just let me know. And seriously, call if you need anything."

I waited while Patrick walked him downstairs and then locked up the house while I stared at the bed. While the photos and the creepy note had been removed, it didn't erase the feeling of being violated that lingered in the room. It seemed that even with my husband being dead, nothing could keep him from continuing to haunt me. While it wasn't clear *who* had been here and left the message for me, it was very clear what this was about.

They knew I murdered my husband.

Twenty-Three

Patrick

I finished securing the house and then carried Travis upstairs with me. He seemed okay, but had been limping, so I didn't want to risk him hurting himself more before I could take him to the vet. He was alert and calm for once, which was a bit odd for him. Thankfully, he was still alive and seemed to be enjoying the pampering as he licked my face repeatedly until we got upstairs.

Poppy was sitting on the floor beside the bed, staring at it. I couldn't begin to imagine what she was feeling right now. I was pissed that someone had been inside my cabin, but I was furious that they'd left the message for her that they did. Someone was purposely fucking with her head, and I was determined to find them and make them pay.

I set him down and smiled when he lay down and closed his eyes, loving the warmth of the carpet from the heater vent. He was a good dog—furniture chewing aside, and it seemed I was actually rather fond of the little guy after all.

Poppy looked up at me, her face etched with something I couldn't quite place. I kneeled in front of her and brushed my finger across her cheek.

"We should get some rest," I said softly.

She nodded and then glanced at the bed. I knew I felt violated that someone had been in the cabin, so there was no doubt that Poppy felt the same way. On top of that, they'd spread pictures of her across the bed and labeled her a murderer.

"How about I change the bedding real quick?" I offered. "A fresh comforter, maybe something a little warmer since it's supposed to be a chilly night."

She nodded and started to get up. I stood and extended my hand to help her, loving the warmth of her skin against mine. I wanted nothing more than to hold Poppy in my arms right now and assure her that everything would be alright. I hadn't just fallen for Poppy; I was so far in over my head that I would burn the world down just to keep her safe and happy.

Once I had the bed changed, I pulled the comforter back and waited for her to climb in. She had changed into one of my t-shirts while I was working on the bed, and I couldn't help but notice how much I loved her wearing my clothes. Even with her having all of the new clothes she'd bought in my closet, knowing that she *chose* to wear mine instead sent a jolt straight to my heart.

I checked on Travis one last time before I climbed into bed beside Poppy and turned off the light. I felt her immediately tense beside me and hated that they had ignited this fear inside of her.

"Want me to turn it back on?" I asked softly.

"No. It's okay. I'll be fine."

"It's not a big deal. I can turn it on."

"I don't know why I'm acting this way," she said, sniffling as a tear slid down her cheek. "I've never been afraid of the dark before. I'm a grown woman, for God's sake."

"Being a grown woman has nothing to do with it. Someone broke into the cabin and left a disturbing message for you in the bed they somehow knew you slept in. That's unsettling, Poppy. I won't try to downplay that for you. I hate that we don't know who it was, but I assure you that they won't get close to you again. It's okay to be upset about it. You don't have to hide your emotions from me, Poppy. This is a safe place for you to feel all of the feelings you keep trying to push away. You're always going to be safe with me, baby. I promise."

She looked up at me as her lower lip trembled. Then she closed her eyes, tears rushing down her face as I held her in my arms and let her fall apart the way she needed to.

I didn't know what time it was or how long Poppy and I had been asleep after she drifted off in my arms, but the sound of Travis snarling immediately woke me up. I jolted, my eyes quickly scanning the room as I gently pulled my arm out from beneath Poppy. She stirred slightly, rolling onto her side as I quietly got out of bed and grabbed the gun from my nightstand.

Travis stood, putting his full weight on the front of his body as he cowered and stared at the bedroom door. He snarled louder, this time waking Poppy.

She rolled over, her eyes quickly assessing the situation as she sat up and pulled the blankets with her. I lifted a finger to my lips to tell her to stay quiet as I took a few steps toward the door. Travis stood beside me, continuing to snarl.

Before we got into bed, I'd given Poppy the other gun, making sure both were fully loaded before we went to sleep. It had been a just-in-case precaution that now suddenly seemed necessary. She threw the blankets off as she climbed out of bed and grabbed her gun.

While the thought of someone trying to hurt her raced through my mind, I felt confident that she could handle herself. If Gage was willing to compliment her aim, I did not doubt what she was capable of.

I took a few more steps, moving slowly and keeping my steps light so the floor didn't creak beneath me. While I had installed new carpet when I first moved in, it didn't change the fact that the cabin was old, and the floors still creaked, regardless of how much padding I put down.

I took a deep breath, lowered my shoulders, and glanced at Poppy one last time. She had her gun steady between her hands with a look of confidence on her face that was sexy as fuck. I ignored the heat that rushed through me as I pulled the door open slowly and kept my gun aimed in front of me.

The hallway was empty as I stepped into it with Travis at my side. He kept his guard up, surprising me with how well-behaved he was and with the sudden protective instincts. I walked slowly, checking each room as Poppy followed behind. We worked pretty well together, both moving in silence while having each other's backs.

I was about to check the guest room when I heard a loud bang on the door. I pulled back and swiveled, aiming my gun in that direction as I took the stairs two at a time. This inevitably triggered Travis, who began barking and howling. *So much for staying in stealth mode.*

I ran the rest of the way down the stairs, determined not to let whoever it was get away. I got to the door and blew out a frustrated breath when I remembered that I had boarded it up. I didn't want to look out the window and get shot in the face, given I didn't know who was waiting on the other side of the door.

The banging had been hard to distinguish whether they were trying to break into the house or—

Suddenly, the sound came again, a solid knock before I heard a voice.

"Poppy, this is Officer Kearton. I really need to speak with you," the voice said from the other side.

I tucked my gun behind my back as Poppy rushed down the stairs and stood beside me.

"The door is secured. Give me a minute," I said loudly, recognizing the voice and name of the female police officer who had come to deliver the news about Dale's death.

I quickly worked to pull the wood from the door while Poppy kept her gun aimed and ready, just in case. While they sounded like Officer Kearton, it was hard to know for sure until we saw them. Not only that, there was no telling if she had come willingly on her own—and better yet, why she would come in the middle of the night.

I pulled the board off and looked at Poppy, who nodded before I unlocked the door and pulled it open.

"I'm so sorry to show up unannounced in the middle of the night, but I really need to talk to you," Officer Kearton said. Her eyes were wide as she looked past me to Poppy.

Poppy lowered the gun but didn't put it away as Officer Kearton stepped forward, not coming inside the house but just close enough so we could hear her.

"I haven't been able to stop thinking about what you mentioned about the offshore account Dale had opened with you as the sole beneficiary. I had a friend of mine who lives in Coyote Creek do some digging, and apparently, it wasn't just an offshore account he opened. Several were opened under different business names at a bank in Coyote Creek. Recently, all of them were changed to remove his business partner, as well as his name. You were added as the sole owner instead."

Poppy stepped forward, keeping the gun at her side before tucking it behind her back. Thankfully, Travis had stopped barking and laid quietly beside me.

"I didn't sign any paperwork to be on any accounts," Poppy said, shaking her head. "I only had one account there, and it was a checking account so that I could get direct deposit. The only time I ever stepped foot inside any bank in Coyote Creek was to open it when I first moved there and got hired at the salon."

"Well, it seems you now have several."

"Why would he remove himself from the accounts and leave me as the sole owner?" Poppy asked.

"My guess is because he caught wind of the FBI finding the offshore account. If he were trying to hide funds, then he would need to immediately remove his name from those accounts so they couldn't be linked to them. Worse yet, if you were the only person on the account, he could turn around and try to frame you."

Poppy shook her head as she tried to process the news.

"What does that even mean?" Poppy asked, more to herself than as an actual question.

"It means that Dale crossed someone and now they're going to come for you," Officer Kearton warned.

"Do you know who this business partner is?" I asked, my brows furrowed.

"I do," she said, nodding her head. "He's not someone you want to mess with, Poppy. He's very dangerous. From what I heard, he's known on the streets as Pac—"

Before she could finish her sentence, a bullet pierced through the howling wind, straight through her brain. Her body fell to the ground, blood immediately pooling around it as I shoved the door closed and pulled Poppy against me.

"What the fuck—" Poppy screamed before I clasped a hand over her mouth to stop her.

"Not now. We need to get you somewhere safe," I said, glancing at the blood pooling under the door as Travis stared at it. "Upstairs. Now."

Poppy nodded and then rushed upstairs, taking them quickly as I picked up Travis and followed behind her.

126

Twenty-Four

Patrick

Poppy sat in the shower on a blanket with Travis at her side while I stood by the door with my phone against my ear and gun drawn.

"What the fuck was that sound?" Gage demanded after I answered on the first ring.

"Gunshot."

"Are you guys—"

"We're fine," I answered quickly. "I'll explain later. Get Julie and Daisy to safety now."

"On it."

We hung up, and I looked behind me at Poppy, who was paler than I had seen before.

"Baby, I need you to use my phone and call 911," I said, stepping back and handing it to her. "You need to call and tell them what happened."

"The storm… They won't… She was a victim too… So much blood…"

I looked down, and my heart shattered as I saw Poppy shaking as tears flooded down her face.

"I know, baby. It's going to be okay. I need you to call 911 for me, okay?"

She nodded and then looked down at the phone before moving her fingers over the screen to place the call. She held it in front of her and put it on speakerphone.

"911, what's your emergency?" a woman answered.

"They killed her," Poppy said with a sniffle.

"Who killed whom?"

I reached down and gently took the phone, giving Poppy a reassuring smile as I took it off speakerphone and pressed it to my ear. I quickly realized, in hindsight, that it was a bad idea to ask her to make the call while she was in shock. I gave all of the information I had to the woman on the phone, who assured me they would send help immediately.

We both knew that Officer Kearton was already dead; we just didn't know who killed her.

Once she had what she needed from me, we disconnected the call, and I put my phone away as I sat by the bathroom door and waited for someone to try their luck with me. I had already let my guard down once when I opened the door to Officer Kearton; I wouldn't make that mistake again.

I grabbed a few pillows from the bed and made a makeshift bed for Poppy in the shower. It wasn't the best place, but it was the safest option I had. Thankfully, it was large enough for her to lie down with Travis cuddled up beside her as she fell asleep. The bathroom was the only room in the cabin that didn't have any windows, so the only way they could get to Poppy now was to go through me, and there was no way in hell I would allow that to happen.

Twenty-Five
Poppy

I woke up the next morning in the shower with a headache that wouldn't go away. The events of last night plagued me, making me nauseous as I struggled not to cry anymore. Knowing that Officer Kearton gave her life to try to save mine had been eating away at me all morning.

I had no idea whether Patrick got any sleep last night, but he had dark circles under his eyes as he talked with the police, who had come at some point while I was sleeping. I knew the winter storm was supposed to be bad, but apparently, it hadn't been enough to keep Officer Kearton from coming to warn me.

Travis sat curled up beside me on the couch as I watched the officers out the living room window as they stood there talking to Patrick. He nodded, then looked inside, his eyes meeting mine as he softly smiled. A few minutes later, he came inside, closing the door behind him, but not before I caught a glimpse of the body covered under a black body bag. I swallowed hard, trying to keep from crying.

"She's still out there?" I asked as he sat beside me and gently squeezed my knee.

He nodded, his eyes bloodshot as the exhaustion showed on his face.

"The storm was too bad last night for them to get out here. They had to wait until this morning and just got here about half an hour ago."

"So she just laid out there in the freezing cold—" I stopped and covered my mouth with my hands as I shook my head. "She's dead because of me."

"She's dead because some fucking asshole killed her, Poppy."

"Yeah, because she found out about Dale's business partner and tried to warn me. If she hadn't come out here, they wouldn't have killed her."

My heart dropped when I realized that they had every opportunity to kill me last night, but didn't. They killed her the second she tried to tell me the name of his business partner, almost as if they could hear what she was saying.

"What?" Patrick asked, studying my face. "What's wrong?"

"They didn't try to hurt me last night," I said, looking at him. "They had an opportunity to, but they didn't. They could have aimed past her and shot me instead. They could have barged in and taken me and—"

"The fuck they could have," he growled, nostrils flaring in response.

"You know what I mean, Pat. They could have tried to come for me last night if they wanted to. Instead, they—"

I stopped talking and looked around the room. While we knew someone had broken into the cabin and left the photos and note for me, it never crossed my mind that they could have left stuff behind. What if they planted hidden cameras or microphones so they knew exactly where we were and what we were saying?

Patrick's face changed from confusion to realization as he sighed and looked around.

"I'll make a call," he said before standing up and heading outside.

Twenty minutes later, Patrick came inside, his features rigid and his body tense.

"Let's go pack your stuff," he said loudly, almost as if he wanted someone to hear him.

"What? Why?" I pulled the blanket off my lap and stood up, following him as he went upstairs.

I didn't know who he had called or what they said, but his change in attitude when he returned left me feeling a bit uneasy. Had he finally decided I was more trouble than I was worth?

Once we entered the bedroom, he wrapped me in a hug and pulled me tight against him, nestling his head in the crook of my neck as he spoke softly in my ear.

"You're going to go stay at the inn for a few days, but we're going to say that you're checking into a hotel in town. I'm pretty sure whoever was here bugged the place, so we don't have much time."

He pulled away and gave my arms a gentle squeeze before reaching under the bed and pausing.

My heart skipped a beat as I watched his face, the way he worked his jaw back and forth before reaching further and ripping something off. He grunted a few times, then pulled his arm back, holding a small black thing in his hand. I didn't have to ask to know it was a listening device. He put it on the ground, stepped on it with his boot, smashed it to pieces, then tossed it in the toilet and flushed.

"That might clog your—" I started, but stopped when he shook his head.

I pressed my lips together and watched as he grabbed the suitcase he had originally been reaching for under the bed and pulled it out. He unzipped it as I gathered my stuff from the closet and started filling it.

While I knew we were just pretending that I was going to stay at a hotel, I couldn't help the feeling that ate away at me as if I were leaving him for real. I expected he would come to the inn with me, but I wasn't sure if he wanted to. I had already uprooted his life as it was; I wouldn't blame him for wanting to be done with me.

"The hotel isn't too far from here," he said as he pulled the zipper shut and then set the suitcase on the floor beside the bed. "If you need anything, just call, and I'll be right there."

"Thank you for getting me a room. I appreciate it."

"My pleasure. This way, we know that you're safe and no one will know where you are."

I nodded, realizing that maybe I needed to speak instead. I had no idea what was still in the room, but if we were going to put on a show, we might as well go all out.

"Thank you, I appreciate that. I know my safety is the top priority for both of us right now."

He forced a smile and led the way back down the stairs as he carried the suitcase for me. We stepped outside, and I was relieved that her body had been moved. The blood still stained the ground, reminding me of what happened. But at least her body was no longer there.

Patrick checked in with one of the officers, letting them know which hotel I would be at. We got in his truck, and I hated the feeling of thinking it might be the last time I felt his hands on my body as he helped me inside. Maybe he'd had enough and was leaving me with Gage to deal with instead.

I fastened my seatbelt, mainly for show, as Patrick climbed in and did the same. He started the truck and slowly pulled out onto the snow-covered ground, the sound of snow and leaves crunching beneath us.

I let out a heavy breath and stared at the window, trying to remind myself that whatever happened now was for the best.

136

Twenty-Six
Patrick

"You're not staying?" Poppy asked.

No matter how hard she tried, I could hear the hurt in her voice.

"I think it's for the best that I don't. We want them to believe you're at the hotel, but I expect they'll send someone back to the cabin to make sure you're not here. If there's a way to catch whoever it is, I'm going to. This might be our only chance," I explained, hating that I couldn't hold her and promise her that I wouldn't leave.

"I hate the thought of something happening to you because of me," she muttered, pulling away as she looked at the floor instead of at me.

"I know. But you're safer here."

"You're putting your sister and niece at risk by having me here. I should have gone to the hotel for real instead of just pretending."

"Daisy is going to stay with my parents for the time being, so she's not a concern. Julie is more than capable of taking care of herself—believe me. Gage and Julie will not allow anything to happen to you. Not only are there plenty of guns and ammunition, but there are also cameras all around the property. Gage will know the second someone even *thinks* about setting foot on his property."

"I don't like this at all," she said, releasing a frustrated breath.

"I know, baby. But it's just temporary. We need to find who is responsible for all of this, and this feels like the best way to do it."

She shook her head and shrugged.

"Fine. If you say so."

I let my head fall in defeat, knowing that there was nothing I could say to make her feel better.

"It's just temporary. I promise. I'll check in as often as I can."

She nodded and pressed her lips together. I could tell that she was shutting down, and I hated it. But after talking to my friend Keith, we decided it was for the best. It was obvious they weren't going to stop until they got what they wanted, but we could at least make it harder for them.

I pushed a breath out through my nose to keep from letting my energy get her more upset. I needed to stay calm and collected, which was hard given everything that was going on.

I leaned into her, feeling her out as I slowly extended my arms, offering her a hug if she wanted to accept it. She sighed and stepped closer, allowing herself to rest against my chest as I wrapped my arms around her and held her. I rested my head on top of hers, smelling the soft scent of her shampoo and realizing how much I was going to miss smelling her in the morning when she showered in my bathroom.

"I'd better get going," I said, not wanting to leave even though I knew I needed to.

She looked up at me with sad eyes, and it nearly broke me.

"Okay. I'll talk to you when I talk to you." She shrugged as if she didn't care, but I could see the hurt in her eyes. This was breaking her as much as it was me.

"We'll talk soon. I promise."

I leaned in and kissed her, hating that I didn't know when the next time would be that I would get to do this again.

"I love you," I said as I slowly pulled away, breaking the kiss.

Her eyes widened as the words registered in her brain.

"I do, Poppy. I fucking love you."

She smiled the first real smile I'd seen in days and looked me in the eyes.

"I love you, too."

"Fuck," I hissed, stepping back as I bit down on my fist.

"What?" Poppy asked with a giggle I hadn't heard in far too long.

"I knew I loved you, but hearing *you* say you love *me* seriously did something," I admit, feeling the strain of my cock in my jeans.

Poppy arched her eyebrows in confusion until she glanced down and noticed.

"Pat!" she shrieked, smacking my arm before looking out the bedroom door to see if anyone was around. "You're so bad!"

"Hey, it's not my fault. You said you love me, and it made my heart grow ten sizes," I teased.

"That's not your *heart*. That's your *cock*."

"Eh, everything grows thanks to you loving me."

She shook her head and tried to hide her smile, but failed.

I glanced at my watch and groaned.

"Shit. I'd better get going. I love you, and I'll talk to you soon. Try to be good while I'm gone, okay?"

"I'll do my best."

I leaned in and gave her one final kiss before leaving, hoping it wouldn't be a big mistake to leave her there. While I knew that Gage and Julie were more than capable of protecting themselves, I didn't trust that whoever was after Poppy wouldn't somehow slip past all of us.

Twenty-Seven

Poppy

It had been a week since I had been staying with Gage and Julie, and during that time, I had only seen Pat twice. I hated the feeling that settled deep inside, telling me that whatever fleeting romance we once shared was now over.

While I had been against staying with my cousin because I didn't want to inconvenience them or bring trouble to their doorstep, I found that it was rather comfortable at the inn. Everything was decorated for Christmas, and there was the warm, homey feel that I had remembered loving about the inn when my grandparents ran it. Even with all of the updates and renovations, it still felt like the safe space I had come to love growing up.

It was a Friday night, and I was feeling restless, so I stayed in my room, curled up on the bed, trying to read a book so I didn't bother Gage and Julie with my sour mood. It wasn't that I wanted to get out of the inn and go somewhere else—it was that I wanted to see Patrick and, for whatever reason, I couldn't. He'd been secretive about what he was doing and why he couldn't come around. I tried pressing Gage to see if he would tell me, but they seemed as tight as they had been when we were growing up, which meant I wasn't going to get anything out of him.

I flipped the page, realizing I didn't know what was happening in the book because I was so distracted. All I could think about was Patrick and how much I missed him. We'd said we loved each other for the first time right before he left, which was frustrating because we didn't even get to celebrate the moment. Not that most couples celebrate it, but Patrick had gotten really hard after I said it, and that was worth celebrating.

I closed the book and tossed it on the nightstand, letting out a sigh of frustration when my phone vibrated. I picked it up and felt the corners of my lips turn up into a smile when I saw a new text message from Patrick.

Patrick: I miss you.

My smile widened as my fingers flew across the screen to respond.

Me: I miss you too. Probably too much.

Dots bounced across the screen as he typed. I loved that he was apparently free right now and that I had his attention.

Patrick: There's no such thing as too much. I miss you a lot, too, baby.

Me: It would be better if you were here.

Patrick: I know. I hate being away from you, too.

Me: It's a week until Christmas, and all I can think about is how you're not here to stuff my stocking.

I waited as the screen showed the bouncing dots, then they'd stop. Then they'd start and stop again. Finally, a message came through.

Patrick: Are you by yourself?

Me: Yes.

Me: Do you want to sneak in, and we can fool around like reckless teenagers?

Patrick: Umm…. No. I don't need Gage putting a bullet in my ass.

Me: Yikes. Yeah, I didn't think about that. He might think you're an intruder since we're constantly expecting one.

Patrick: He'd do it just for the hell of it because I touched you.

Me: Well, lucky for us, we've practically gone back to virgin status, given how long it's been since we've touched each other.

My phone rang, startling me when I saw a FaceTime call from Patrick. I tucked my hair behind my ears and answered it.

"I take it someone is feeling a little frustrated tonight," he teased, looking far too sexy sitting on his bed without me. His hair was wet, and I knew that if I closed my eyes, I could smell the scent of his shampoo as if I were there with him.

"I've been *more* than a little frustrated for a while now," I admitted, getting comfortable against the headboard and adjusting the tank top that I decided to sleep in.

Given that we hadn't seen or heard anything since the night of the shooting at the cabin, I'd given up on trying to wear something appropriate in case I had to run for my life in the middle of the night. I'd been hot and restless, so tonight I was focused on comfort for once.

"Go lock your door," he said, his jaw fixed as he waited for me to do as he said.

"Why? Is the big, bad wolf going to come eat me?"

"No, but I'll take note of that little fantasy the next time I see you. Now go lock the door, Poppy."

His tone was stern, sending a flush of heat through my body. I didn't like anyone else bossing me around, but having Patrick's take-charge attitude in the bedroom could set me on fire.

I rolled my eyes as I got up and did as he asked.

"Happy?" I asked, walking back to the bed.

"Almost. Show me what you're wearing."

I cocked my head and pinned him with a look.

"You show me what you're wearing first."

"Fine," he said, his gaze heating as he lowered his phone.

My thighs clenched, and my pussy ached as he slowly moved it, showing me his toned abs before stopping at his boxer briefs. I felt my mouth water the second I saw the thick outline of his hard cock through them.

"You cheat," I hissed as he lifted the phone and showed his face again.

"Why? I'm just sitting here, being comfy after taking a shower."

"No, you're sitting there wearing practically nothing while showing me the cock I want that you won't give me."

"Soon, baby," he promised. "But for now, let me take care of you and help with that frustration."

"And how exactly are you going to do that from there?"

"Easy. I'm going to talk you through it, and you're going to make yourself come for me."

My eyebrows shot up my forehead as a flush of heat rushed over my skin. I knew the blush covered my neck and cheeks by the grin he was sporting.

"I've never done this before," I stammered, not knowing what else to say.

"That's okay. We'll take our time. We've got all night, baby."

"Okay." I pushed out a quick breath through my pursed lips, trying to force out the nerves that threatened to take over.

"Take your shorts and panties off."

"How do you know I'm wearing shorts?"

"I know you too well, Poppy. I can tell by the tank top that you're hot and uncomfortable. When you get like that, you like to wear your loose pink booty shorts. Now take them off."

I glanced down, shaking my head that he was right. Those were exactly what I was wearing.

"I need to set you down for a minute," I said, getting ready to lay the phone on the bed.

"Prop your phone up against the lamp and let me watch."

A shiver ran through me at the thought of taking my clothes off in front of him while on FaceTime. I'd done some crazy shit in my life, but this was never part of it.

I debated for half a second before saying fuck it and setting the phone up so he could see me. Then I slowly hooked my thumbs into the waistband of my shorts and pulled them down my legs.

"You're wearing a fucking thong," he noted, groaning as his eyes stayed fixed on the screen.

I grinned and turned in a slow circle, making sure he got a good look at my ass before bending over and spreading my legs slightly. I didn't know what had come over me, but I loved the way he was making me feel right now. Powerful and wanted and sexy—all at the same time.

"Fuck, baby. Look at how wet you are," he continued. "Your pussy is drenched, Poppy."

I took my time standing straight as I turned around and faced him, my hand slowly slipping beneath my panties as he watched.

"Tell me how wet it is."

I widened my stance slightly, then pushed my panties to the side so he could see as I slid a finger inside. I closed my eyes and gasped, my body already on fire just from his words.

"I'm so wet," I moaned quietly as I slid another finger in. "Fuck, Pat. I wish it were your fingers instead."

"Me too, baby. I wish it were my fingers and my tongue and my cock."

"I fucking miss your cock."

"He misses you, too."

"Show me," I said, catching myself off guard by how bold I was.

He grinned and lowered the top of his boxer briefs as he pulled his cock out and stroked it.

"Is this what you want to see?"

"Yes," I whimpered, getting closer to the phone as I watched him touch himself.

A dot of precum glistened on the tip before he smoothed his finger over it and wiped it away.

"Take your panties off, baby. Lie down on the bed and spread your legs for me."

I grabbed the phone and did as he asked.

"Show me how you touch yourself."

I flipped the camera view so he could see my hand as it feathered over my bare pussy before sliding a finger inside. I could still see his cock as he stroked it slowly, watching as I slid my finger deeper inside. I pulled it out, showing him how it glistened with my arousal before sliding it back inside and inserting another.

"Fuck, Poppy. You make me want to come just seeing you touch yourself."

"You make me want to come," I admitted, loving how turned on I was for him.

"Rub your clit," he coaxed as he stroked himself faster.

The thought of sucking his dick made me moan as I pressed my middle finger firmly against my clit and began rubbing. I could feel the way the thick vein in the underside of his cock felt against my tongue as I pictured him fucking my face and making me gag as I took him to the back of my throat.

"Fuck, baby. Yeah. Just like that. Faster. Faster."

I listened to his words, increasing my speed as I closed my eyes and felt the first spasm as I clenched my thighs together and shook as an earth-shattering orgasm tore through me.

When I opened my eyes, I flipped the camera so it was in selfie mode again, and grinned when I saw the cum on his chest.

 I panted hard as I pulled my finger out, and my body sagged against the bed.

"Better?" he asked, looking as relaxed as I felt.

"Somewhat. I still don't have your cock inside of me, so there's that."

"Soon enough, my love. Soon enough."

"You say that, but then we never get to actually see each other. I'm starting to think this was all for nothing. It doesn't seem like anyone is watching me, nor does anyone even know that I exist anymore. I say we call it a day and go back to how things were before."

"We can't risk it, Poppy," he said softly. "I don't trust that this is over. We just have to be patient and wait for them to make a mistake. Then we can end things on our terms."

I sighed heavily, allowing my shoulders to drop as a big yawn escaped me.

"Try to get some rest," he said, wrapping up our call.

"You too. I'll talk to you when I talk to you, I guess."

"Goodnight, Poppy," he said, not feeding into the spiral I was sure to go down, given how tired I was.

"Goodnight."

I hung up the call, got dressed, and then climbed into bed. While I was still frustrated that I couldn't be with Patrick, I knew that I would sleep a tad bit better now that some of my frustration had been worked out.

Twenty-Eight
Patrick

Having phone sex with Poppy was fun, but it was nothing compared to actually being with her. Not having her in my house for a week had created a depression for both Travis and me, or at least that's what I told myself when he refused to do anything but lie on the couch where she liked to sit. Thankfully, he seemed to recover quickly from whatever happened to him, and the vet gave him a clean bill of health once I finally took him in.

I'd been working with Keith on trying to set up some sort of trap to catch whoever had been stalking Poppy. Whoever it was seemed well-versed in staying below the radar, because nothing I did worked. I thought for sure my friend who worked at the hotel would report back to me that someone had asked about Poppy and which room she was in, but no one came in. It was strange and continued to gnaw at me as I struggled to figure out what their next move would be.

It was less than a week until Christmas, and I needed to finish my shopping. I desperately wanted to ask Poppy to go with me, but I knew that wasn't safe. We needed her to stay as hidden as possible until we could identify the threat before they got to her. I knew it had to be driving her crazy staying cooped up at the inn, but Gage assured me that Poppy and Julie were getting along beautifully and that Poppy seemed to be having a nice time.

I picked up my phone and pressed it to my ear, checking my watch to make sure it wasn't too early. While Gage was usually an early riser, it was a Saturday morning, and they didn't have Daisy, which meant he might be sleeping in.

On the third ring, he answered.

"What's up?"

"Hey, I was heading into town to finish my Christmas shopping and grab supplies before this storm hits. Just thought I would check in and see if you wanted to go stock up, too," I said, looking out the window as the snow fell lightly.

"Actually, I was just getting ready to call you. I was planning to head out in ten minutes if that works for you?"

"Sounds good," I said, taking a moment to build up the courage to ask for a favor. "Hey, since I'm going to be at the store anyway, can you check with Poppy and see if she wants or needs anything? I know it's probably frustrating her that she can't go on her own, but I figured the least I can do is grab stuff for her while I'm there."

"Yeah, let me ask her real quick and then I'll call you back."

"Sounds good."

I hung up the phone and lifted the coffee mug to my lips, taking a sip. Mornings without Poppy just weren't the same. It was funny how quickly her presence here had already changed things for me, especially when I found myself reaching for a bag of mini Oreos this morning for breakfast, knowing they were her favorite.

A few minutes later, Gage called back.

"Did you get a list?" I asked, already knowing that Poppy would have something she wanted. She liked to shop, and I loved that about her. Even though she had acted as if she hated it when I took her the first day she was here, I could see the excitement on her face as she relaxed and started shopping.

"I did, and surprisingly, it's more than just Oreos."

"We can't have her not having her Oreos," I teased, chuckling, before saying goodbye so I could get my stuff together and leave. I pulled my jacket on, checked to make sure the baby gate was up to keep Travis out of my bed while I was gone, then grabbed my keys and left.

When I parked in front of the inn, it took everything inside of me not to run in and see Poppy. The goal was to keep her hidden, just in case they didn't know she was staying there. Given there hadn't been any sign of them since the night they murdered Officer Kearton, it was hard to know what they knew and what they didn't. For now, we had to act like they didn't know where Poppy was and pray we were right.

A few minutes later, Gage came out and got in the truck, waving to Julie through the window as she watched us leave. I glanced at the bedroom where I knew Poppy was staying, and my heart sank when I didn't see her there. It was for the better, I reminded myself as I pulled away and headed into town.

154

Twenty-Nine

Poppy

I stared out the sheer curtains and watched as Patrick drove away. It killed me not to open them and wave, but I knew that the goal was for me to stay as hidden as possible, so I didn't risk it.

Shortly after they left, Julie and I were in the kitchen when we heard a knock at the front door. We both exchanged a panicked look as I grabbed a knife from the block and hid behind the corner as she went to answer the door.

I peeked around the wall, and my heart dropped when I recognized the male officer who had come out to the cabin to tell me that Dale's body had been found. He was dressed in uniform and clutched an envelope with my name on it in his hands in front of him.

"I'm sorry to bother you, ma'am," he said loud enough I could hear him. "I am trying to locate Poppy Grant. There didn't appear to be anyone at the cabin where she was staying, so I thought I would check here. Have you by chance seen her?"

Julie glanced over her shoulder, and I could tell she was unsure what to do.

I set the knife down and walked out, pulling my shoulders back as I approached. While it was a bold and probably risky move to make myself seen, I couldn't stop wondering what was in the envelope.

"Hi," I said as I approached.

Julie smiled and stepped back, allowing me to stand in front of him.

"Mrs. Grant," he said and smiled. "We received the autopsy report for Dale Hudson, and I wanted to make sure you received a copy. I know that this was something that was important for Officer Kearton, and so I wanted to do this on her behalf."

"I'm so sorry for your loss," I whispered, my eyes stinging with tears.

His eyes became glossy as well, but he was much quicker than I was at pushing his emotions away and regaining control.

"Thank you. She was the best partner that I could have ever asked for and will be greatly missed."

I nodded and pressed my lips into the best smile I could muster.

"Thank you for dropping this off. I appreciate it."

"My pleasure."

He turned and walked away as I closed and locked the door behind him. My fingers trembled as I held the envelope in my hands, staring at it.

"Want to open it together?" Julie offered, standing beside me.

"Yes," I said quickly, my nerves already getting the best of me.

I was shocked they had the report so quickly, especially since online it said it could take weeks to months. But then again, it wasn't that big of a surprise given that he worked in law enforcement and was being investigated by the FBI. There were several people who wanted immediate answers on what happened to him.

My heart raced as I tore open the envelope and pulled the paper out. I scanned it, my brain too rushed to actually read the full report. I didn't need to know all of the details about Dale; I just needed to see what they ruled as the cause of death.

Julie looked over my shoulder, both of us reading quietly as I tried to process what everything meant. There were several notes about blunt force trauma, which I knew was from me hitting him with the pan. Then I got to the part where it stated that numerous tests confirmed he appeared to be under the influence of alcohol at the time of the accident and that it was estimated that he had a BAC of .22 or higher.

The official cause of death was listed as asphyxia due to drowning with blunt force trauma to the head, and acute ethanol intoxication was a significant contributing factor to the accident and subsequent death. The manner of death showed the word *accident*.

I gasped and covered my mouth as I turned and looked at Julie.

"They think his death was an accident," I said quietly, still not believing what I read. "But they found blunt force trauma, so that means they're going to look into it, right? I mean, the car didn't have any damage to it, so it's not like he hit a tree and hurt his head that way. They're going to know that I killed him, that *I* was the one who caused the trauma to his head."

I could feel the panic rushing through me as I processed everything.

Julie gently placed her hands on my arms and looked me in the eyes.

"It's okay, Poppy. Who's to say that he wasn't drunk before he got in the car and that he didn't fall and hit his head somewhere in the house? Drunk people stumble and fall all the time. Plus, we don't know what they found with the search warrant once they entered the house. You said it yourself that you washed off the pans and put them away before you left. He wasn't bleeding, so it wasn't like there was a trail of blood from you dragging his body to the garage. I don't think they're going to suspect you. You also put in the police report that you filed here that he had been drinking the night he attacked you. There's a record of his intoxication *before* his fatal accident. I think you're overthinking this."

I nodded and let out a slow, unsteady breath as my body trembled.

"Until the cops come to question you about his death, I think it's safe to say that this chapter is closed. Try not to stress about it unless you have to."

"You're right. I don't know why I keep trying to freak myself out over everything."

"Because this is a lot, Poppy. I get it, and I'm not trying to disregard your feelings one bit. I just think that for now, we don't have to worry about this. Let's let the dust settle and see what happens next."

"Sounds like a plan," I agreed, taking a deep breath.

Julie's phone started ringing, and part of me hoped that it was Gage letting her know they were headed back. While I knew I couldn't see Patrick right now, I felt better knowing he was just a cabin away from me. Silver Falls had gotten lucky with the past few storms blowing right past us, but the next one was guaranteed to hit us spot on. According to the local meteorologist, this storm could break the record for the worst storm ever to hit Silver Falls.

I'd heard Gage and Julie talking this morning about stocking up on supplies and making sure her parents had what they needed for Daisy. I hated that they couldn't be with Daisy because I was here, but we didn't have a lot of options. Julie assured me that it was better for Daisy to stay with her parents because they were in Silver Falls and could get what she needed more easily than Julie could, being stuck at the inn. The roads leading back to town would definitely be impacted, and we would be trapped back here until the storm let up enough for them to try to plow them.

"I'm sorry, I need to take this real quick," Julie said, smiling as she lifted the phone to her ear. "Hey, Mom. What's up?"

I sat on the couch and set the report on the coffee table as I tried to force myself to relax.

"Are you serious? How long has she been running a fever?" Julie paused where she was as she listened, the concern of a mother worried about her daughter etched across her face. "Shit. I can call Gage and—"

She tipped her head back in frustration and groaned.

"Go," I said softly, pulling her attention to me. "Go to your daughter. I'll be fine. No one knows I'm here, and if anyone comes for me, I have plenty of weapons to choose from here."

"Hold on for a second," Julie said to her mom before turning the phone away from her face so she didn't speak into it as she talked to me. "Are you sure? I don't want to—"

I held up a hand to stop her.

"Yes, I'm sure. Go take care of your daughter. I'll be just fine."

She blew out a heavy, frustrated breath and then started talking to her mother again. A few seconds later, she hung up and grabbed her jacket from the coat rack.

"I won't be gone long," she assured me as she put it on and grabbed her keys. "Daisy spiked a fever out of nowhere and has a rash that my mom is worried about. I might need to take her to the doctor while I'm there, but I promise, I'll be back as soon as I can. I'll call Gage and tell them to hurry back as well."

"You should take Duke with you. I'm sure it would cheer her up to see her best friend. I'm just going to sit here and eat my Oreos while binge-watching some holiday movies. Don't worry about me." I smiled as I grabbed the remote and turned on the TV.

Julie nodded, more to herself than me, then left and locked the door behind her as Duke followed her.

I flipped through the channels, knowing there was no way I was going to sit and watch a movie. My brain was too distracted for any of that. So I put on something that felt Christmassy and grabbed my phone, opened the tab I had been looking at earlier, and resumed my search for places to live in California.

162

Thirty
Patrick

While we had been quick to gather the supplies we needed for the storm, I was taking my time finding the stuff Poppy had asked for. It wasn't much, mainly some snacks that made me grin because I could picture her sitting on the couch with her messy bun, wearing my t-shirt, and munching on Oreos.

Gage walked beside me, stopping for a second to pull his phone out of his pocket. He glanced at the screen and then swiped his finger across it to answer it.

"Hey, baby. What's up?"

We continued walking with me pushing our shopping cart while he talked to my sister.

"Is she okay?" he asked, and I immediately stopped, the blood whooshing in my ears as my heart sank.

He covered the mouthpiece with his hand quickly to speak to me.

"Daisy has a rash and a fever, so Julie is heading to the condo to check on her," he explained before returning his attention to the phone call. "Do you need me to grab anything while I'm here?"

I hated the thought that Daisy was sick as much as I hated the idea that Poppy was at the inn by herself. Even if she needed one of us, it would be thirty to forty-five minutes before we could get to her. I gripped the shopping cart handle tightly, my knuckles turning white before I gave in and pulled out my phone.

It wasn't that I *wasn't* supposed to be talking to Poppy. It was that I hated that our relationship had been reduced to text messages, and it killed me that I couldn't go see her. I wanted to touch her and hold her and make love to her. But for now, a text would have to suffice so I could make sure she was okay.

Me: Hey, I heard Julie needed to leave to check on Daisy. Are you okay?

I pulled the cart to the side of the aisle so people could get past us easily as I waited for the dots to appear on the screen to show that she was responding. A second later, they appeared.

Poppy: I'm fine. Just sitting on the couch, watching holiday movies.

Me: Bullshit.

A grin pulled across my face as I watched the screen, waiting for her response. In the short time I'd gotten to know Poppy, I knew that sitting down and watching a cheesy holiday movie was not her cup of tea. It wouldn't surprise me if by the time Gage and Julie got back, Poppy had redecorated the entire inn for them. She got restless easily, and I loved how we used to handle that restless energy.

Poppy: Are you calling me a liar?

Me: Yes.

Poppy: The nerve...

Me: Prove it.

I felt Gage's eyes on me, but I ignored it as he continued his conversation with Julie and I had a few minutes to chat with Poppy. Then a picture message came through, and I about lost it.

Poppy was sitting on the couch at the inn, wearing nothing but my t-shirt, her legs spread wide as she chewed her nail, looking at the camera. The shirt was pulled up just enough to give me a glimpse of her pussy, which made it even hotter.

Me: I fucking miss you.

Poppy: I miss fucking you.

I grinned and shook my head. She was going to be the death of me.

Me: I'm officially inviting myself over to dinner at the inn tonight. I'll see you as soon as I can.

Poppy: I'll be waiting.

I put my phone away and made it my mission to rush through grabbing the rest of the stuff we needed so I could get back to Poppy sooner.

Thirty-One
Poppy

I got dressed quickly after sending the naughty photo to Patrick, just in case Julie was already on her way back. She hadn't been gone long, but I didn't want to risk her showing up and me sitting naked on their couch as I sent dirty messages to my cousin's best friend.

I pulled on a hoodie after feeling chilly and debated putting on my fleece-lined leggings instead of the loose sweatpants I was wearing. I couldn't figure out why I had suddenly gotten so cold, especially when they liked to keep the inn nice and toasty.

My stomach rumbled, reminding me that I hadn't had any real food to eat today, besides my Oreos. I walked into the kitchen and was rummaging through the fridge when I heard a knock on the front door. I paused, freezing as I debated whether to run and hide or to be brave and face whoever was on the other side of the door.

I grabbed the knife I had left out earlier after the cop left and clutched it at my side as I walked to the door, stopping suddenly when I saw who was there. Her blond hair was unmistakable as she shivered and looked around, stepping back from the door as she waited for someone to answer it.

I set the knife down and rushed over, pulling it open as a gust of cold air rushed in.

"Lisa? What are you doing here?" I asked.

I hadn't talked to her since the day I called her to let her know I'd left town and that I didn't know when or if I would be back to work at the salon.

"Hey, Poppy," she said with a warm smile, her jaw chattering as she struggled against the cold. "Mind if I come in for a few? It is freezing out here."

"Yeah, sure," I replied, stepping back to let her in before closing the door. "But why are you here?"

I was so confused because it wasn't like Lisa and I had been super close. I worked for her, but we were never what I would call *friends*. Not that she wasn't a nice person—she was. We just never crossed that line with me being her employee.

"I came to check on you," she said, the features on her face shifting slightly as her fingers fidgeted inside the sleeves of her puffy coat.

"Oh. Well, that was nice of you…"

Then it hit me.

I never told Lisa where I was when I called her. She specifically told me not to.

"How did you know I was—"

In the blink of an eye, she reached her hand into her coat

pocket, pulled out a syringe, and then jammed the needle into my neck. I gasped as my mind and heart raced, the fear washing over me as quickly as whatever she had just injected into my system.

A malicious grin spread across her face as she finger-waved at me before everything went black and I hit the floor.

Thirty-Two

Patrick

"FUCK!" Gage growled, leaning forward in his seat as he stared at his phone.

"What's wrong?" I asked, glancing at him before returning my attention to the road. It seemed the storm was fully upon us now, with heavy blankets of snow falling around me. Visibility had decreased to pretty much nothing, so I had to hope and pray that I could see enough to find the main road back to the inn.

"Someone's at the inn."

"What the fuck do you mean *someone's at the inn*?"

"I mean someone is at the fucking inn, and Poppy just let her in."

"Do you recognize the person?"

"No. Not at all. She has blond hair but refuses to look at the camera, so I can't see her face. Puffy coat makes it hard to see anything else."

"Is anyone with her?" I asked, desperate to know everything I could.

"Not that I see."

"Do you have any cameras inside the house? Can you check those and see what's happening?"

"No. We don't have cameras inside."

"Fuck." I gripped the steering wheel tighter and pressed the gas, needing to get to her faster.

"We can't do anything for her if we're dead," he warned. "We have to trust that it's someone she knows if she let them in the house."

"I don't trust anyone when it comes to keeping Poppy safe," I answered, letting off the gas because he was right—we couldn't do anything if we were dead. But I also couldn't stand the thought that Poppy could get hurt—or worse, killed.

I exhaled the breath I hadn't realized I'd been holding when I finally saw the sign for the road that led back to the inn. I checked both directions before pulling out onto the main highway and taking the turn I needed.

"How well do you know this road?" Gage asked, looking at me with a look I never wanted to see again in my life. His face was etched in worry and fear as anger clenched his jaw.

"Better than I know myself. Why?"

"Because whoever it was had help and they just dragged Poppy out of the house, so you better fucking get there *now*."

My jaw tightened as I pressed my foot to the pedal and prayed that we could get to her before it was too late.

Thirty-Three
Poppy

My head throbbed when I opened my eyes and looked around, no idea where I was. Lisa immediately came into view as she stared at me with something that felt like disgust.

"She's awake," she said to someone over her shoulder before stepping back and folding her arms over her chest.

"It's about time," a male voice answered.

I tried to sit up, my body weak and my head disoriented. Then he came into view, and my heart stopped as I realized who it was. He wasn't wearing the uniform he had on earlier when he delivered the autopsy report, but his face was unmistakable. He was Officer Kearton's partner.

"We don't have much time. We need the passwords to the bank accounts, and you're going to give them to us," he said, standing in front of me as he stared into my eyes, his dark and narrow.

"I… I don't have any passwords," I stammered, looking from him to Lisa.

"Don't fucking play with me," he warned.

"I'm not. I have no idea what accounts you're talking about."

"Really?" Lisa asked, stepping forward and glaring at me. "Don't play stupid, Poppy. It doesn't look good on you."

"I seriously don't know what accounts you guys are talking about. I only have one bank account, and I'm pretty sure it's overdrawn at this point. I can give you the—"

"Enough!" Officer Hughes boomed, his name coming to me as I recalled seeing it pinned to his uniform earlier. "Cut the bullshit and just give us the information!"

I held my hands in front of me, staring at both of them. I shook my head, then realized my whole body was shaking. It was no doubt due to the lack of food today, combined with the stress of being kidnapped and getting yelled at for something I didn't have answers to.

Lisa grabbed a laptop and slammed it down on the table beside me. The room wasn't very big, and I still had no idea where it was. But there was a lamp on the table beside me that was turned on, so wherever it was had electricity, which made me think it wasn't just a random abandoned place in the middle of nowhere. She pulled up the online banking website and turned the computer to face me.

"Put the information in *now*," she snarled, shoving it at me.

"Lisa, I swear to God, I don't know—"

Before I could finish my sentence, she backhanded me across the face, sending my head back against the hard wall. The pain immediately flooded through me as I blinked and tried to focus.

"I'm not *fucking playing,* Poppy. Dale went in, removed himself and the other person from the account, and added you. I want to know why," Lisa said, her face red with anger.

"I don't know why he would do that. He never said anything to me about any of this. If I had the information, I would give it to you. But I don't."

"Then I suggest we call and get it," she sneered, pulling out her phone and swiping her finger across the screen before pressing the speakerphone button.

A few seconds later, an automated message for the Coyote Creek Bank filled the silence. I watched as she pressed the button to speak to a customer service representative.

"When they answer, you're going to tell them that you need to set up online banking for all of the accounts you're listed on," Lisa said quickly. "Do you understand me?"

I nodded, hoping that it was already past closing time and no one would be there this late on a Saturday. It had been forever since I'd gone into the bank, so I didn't even know what their business hours were today. Unfortunately, luck was *not* on my side when a woman answered a few minutes later.

"Thank you for calling Coyote Creek Bank. This is Sasha. How may I help you?"

Lisa raised her eyebrows and shoved her phone toward me, demanding that I speak.

"Hi, ummm... yes, I need help… um… setting up…" I paused for a moment, too panicked to get my words out.

Officer Hughes pulled a gun out from behind his back and stepped closer, pressing it against my temple. I closed my eyes and felt my jaw tremble with fear.

"I'm sorry, I didn't quite get that. What did you need help with?" Sasha asked.

"Online banking," I rushed out, opening my eyes to find Lisa and Officer Hughes watching me. "I have a few accounts that I need to set up online banking for."

"I can help with that. Do you have the account numbers?"

"I do not. Are you able to look me up by name?"

"Absolutely. What name would they be under?"

"Poppy Grant," I answered.

"Please give me a moment while I pull up the accounts."

I nodded, though she couldn't see me. While I verified my information, Lisa grabbed a piece of paper and scribbled a note. She turned it to me, and I read it, giving her a thumbs up in acknowledgment because what else could I do? There was a gun pressed against my head; it wasn't like I was in any position to say no to their requests.

"I show that you already have online access for one of the accounts, but if you can give me a few minutes, I'll set up the others."

"Thank you. I appreciate it."

"Would you like to link the accounts so you can transfer online between them?"

Lisa nodded, so I confirmed.

"If it's possible, can you please confirm the balance in each account for me?" I asked, trying to find a way to incorporate Lisa's demand, which she had written on the paper, without it feeling out of place.

"Of course. Let me finish setting the last account up, and I'll get those balances for you."

"Thank you."

We waited a few minutes for Sasha to finish setting up the accounts before she gave me the temporary login information, which Lisa immediately wrote down.

Sasha came back on the line and began giving me the balance information in all of the accounts. While I wasn't surprised that my account only had seven dollars in it, my jaw dropped when I heard the thousands of dollars that were sitting in the other accounts. I had no clue what Dale was involved with or how he had accumulated all of this money. What was even more disturbing was that he'd added me to these accounts, as well as the offshore one the FBI was investigating. Thanks to him, I was now the sole owner of several fraudulent accounts, with my boss and a local police officer threatening me to get the money I never even knew about until now.

Lisa scribbled another note and then shoved it at me, glaring as she waited for me to do it.

"Um, thank you for the balances," I said nervously. "Is it possible to make a few transfers to another account while I have you on the phone?"

"Absolutely. What account would you like to start with?"

I read off the number for the one Lisa pointed to, then read the account number she wrote beside it. The name listed for that account was Jason Hughes. I felt a shiver creep up my spine as I realized what was happening. She was transferring the money to Officer Hughes.

"Okay, I have that account pulled up. How much would you like to transfer?"

Lisa mouthed *all of it* to me, so I sighed and confirmed.

We finished the remaining transfers, moving everything from the accounts Dale had set up to Officer Hughes' account. I knew it had to look weird and hoped Sasha would report it as soon as she finished the call so they could freeze his accounts and keep him from using it. Once we had confirmation that the transfers were complete, Officer Hughes lowered the gun, tucked it into the back of his jeans, and grabbed the laptop.

Lisa pressed the button to end the call, not bothering to let me thank Sasha for her help. Then she stood over Officer Hughes's shoulder and watched as he logged into his bank account and grinned at the large balance in it. I tried to watch what was happening without them knowing and leaned slightly to the side until I could see the screen.

He opened another browser, and an offshore bank appeared on the screen. His fingers flew quickly over the keyboard as he entered his login information, then my breath hitched in my throat when I saw the name listed on the account: *Paco H. Lopez.*

A flashback slammed into my brain of the night Officer Kearton came to the cabin, warning me of the danger I was in.

"It means that Dale crossed someone and now they're going to come for you," Officer Kearton warned.

"Do you know who this business partner is?" Patrick

asked, his brows furrowed.

"I do," she said, nodding her head. "He's not someone you want to mess with, Poppy. He's very dangerous. From what I heard, he's known on the streets as Pac—"

Fuck.

It turned out Lisa wasn't just my controlling boss at the salon. She was working with Dale's business partner, who just happened to be a police officer in Silver Falls.

Thirty-Four
Patrick

By the time I got to the inn, Gage and I were thankful to be alive. That storm was a fucking disaster, with strong wind gusts threatening to flip my truck and thick layers of snow reducing visibility to nothing. I was surprised we got through it in one piece, but then again, there was nothing that could stand in my way of getting to Poppy.

I threw the truck in park, jumped out of the cab, and ran to the front door, struggling to catch my breath in the harsh wind. My heart hammered in my chest, my blood pressure soaring as I raced through the inn, desperate to find Poppy. My heart sank as I fought off the urge to scream, knowing she was gone. There wasn't any sign of struggle, but that did nothing to reassure me that she was okay.

Gage came in behind me, both of us abandoning our stuff in the covered bed of the truck as he talked to Julie on the phone. She hadn't been able to make it back before the storm hit, so she was going to stay with her parents and keep an eye on Daisy.

My phone rang, and I whipped it out of my pocket so fast that I nearly dropped it. I swiped my finger across the screen to answer it, not bothering to check the caller ID.

"Hello," I said, gripping it tight as I prayed it was her.

"Hey. We know where she is," Keith said, cutting straight to it. I loved that about him.

I had Gage call him the second we knew Poppy was gone, and he assured me he was on it.

"Fuck. Thank God. Where is she?"

"It looks like they have her in a cabin not far from the inn," he confirmed as I heard a keyboard clicking in the background.

What was it with these fucking cabins? Was this just the place *that lunatics liked to take their victims to torture them? Was there some secret Silver Falls fight club, and everyone knew to come to the woods and find an abandoned cabin to do their dirty work?*

"Where at?" I asked, shoving a hand through my hair as Gage ended his call and listened to mine.

"I'm not sure exactly. We're trying to pinpoint an exact location, but the storm is interfering a bit."

"Fine. I'll go driving around until I find her."

"You won't," Keith said firmly. "You're going to stay at the inn, with Gage, and wait for an update from me."

"No. No fucking way," I growled. "I appreciate you finding her general location, but there's no fucking chance that I'm going to just sit this out and wait for someone to go find her."

"I know you care about her deeply, but I need you to hear me when I say this," Keith said slowly. "If you so much as *set foot outside* of that inn, I will come after you for interfering with a federal investigation. I already have men on the ground, searching the area. As soon as I have confirmation of the location, I will go in and extract her. I need you to sit back and allow me to do my job."

"I can't—"

"You will. This isn't optional, Pat. This isn't some romance book where you swoop in and save the day. You can play hero with her after I get her out safely. Until then, sit your ass down and let me do my job."

Before I could say anything else, the line went dead.

184

Thirty-Five
Poppy

I rocked back and forth on the floor with my knees pulled to my chest as Lisa and Officer Hughes talked in the kitchen across from me. They'd tried to move the money from his account to the one listed under Paco, but encountered an error that pissed Officer Hughes off enough that he took his frustration out on the wall, punching several holes in it.

Suddenly, the front door burst open, a gust of wind rushing inside and sending a chill through the small space. My heart raced as I tried to lift my head, hoping it was Patrick or Gage coming to rescue me. But instead, it sank when I looked at the man who stepped inside and closed the door behind him. He glanced down at me, his eyes piercing me with an odd familiarity, before he walked into the kitchen and glared at Lisa and Officer Hughes.

"You had one *fucking* job," he snarled, leaning on the island as he stared at Officer Hughes.

"I know, Dad," Officer Hughes said tightly. "I thought we were well ahead of everything and didn't think they would freeze the account yet."

"Yeah, well, it appears you weren't."

The man turned and walked over to me, pulling out a folding chair and flipping it around as he sat in front of me.

"Hello, Poppy. Nice to see you again. I trust your dinner was good," he said, his voice even as realization hit. He was the man from the restaurant who had been watching me and left the note with the hostess.

My lip trembled as I clutched my knees tighter to my chest, trying to stay warm as a mixture of fear and anxiety rushed through me.

"It seems I know a lot about you, but you don't seem to know anything about me," he continued, his posture poised as if he were a man of sophistication. "It seems my business partner kept his word and didn't tell anyone what we were up to, though I find that hard to believe given that he changed all of our accounts suddenly before he died. Wouldn't you agree that it's a bit strange that he put all of those accounts in *your* name, just days before he was brutally murdered?"

His dark eyes stayed fixed on mine while I swallowed hard. *Murdered. He knew what really happened.*

"I don't know what you're talking about," I said firmly. "I didn't know those accounts existed until about half an hour ago."

He nodded and looked around the room before letting his glare rest on me again.

"I find that hard to believe."

I shrugged the best I could and tried to hide that I was shivering.

"Do you want to know what I think happened?" he pressed, leaning forward and resting his arms over the back of the chair.

I sat there quietly, not responding.

"I think that you found out about the money and joined forces with Dale to cut me out of the deals. I think that once Dale found out that the FBI had found the offshore account, you both agreed to remove him from the other accounts to keep that money safe. If you were the sole owner, you could move quickly and transfer the money into another account with the fake identification he created for you. The only problem was that you killed him before that could happen."

Lisa and Officer Hughes came over and stood behind him as he continued talking.

"You see, I thought I knew Dale, but I was wrong. I thought he was a trustworthy guy and believed him when he said he had a solid plan for the Fentanyl we were moving. He assured me that marrying you would be the best move because you were so desperate to be loved that you would marry anyone. We even worked with Lisa, who hired you and gave you a job, even though she knew your background. We all thought that with your record of embezzlement, you would be an asset to our team. Never once did we think that you would cross all of us."

I glanced at Lisa, trying to read her face. It had seemed like pure luck when she approached me at the diner that day, noting how upset I was when I'd lost my job as a waitress at the local bar. She'd offered me a job on the spot, even though I had zero experience working in a salon. It was an entry-level position where I handled all scheduling, stocking supplies, and basic cleaning, but it was a job. I never would have expected her to have ulterior motives the entire time.

"So, that leaves me with one question," he continued, his body rigid as he sat in front of me. "Where is the information on the new identity that Dale had created for you?"

I looked away from him, not bothering to answer because it didn't matter what I said. I had no idea what he was talking about, and telling him that would only make him angrier.

His nostrils flared as he got up, threw the chair across the room out of his way, then reached down and grabbed me by the throat. He pushed my back against the wall as he lifted me, his fingers tightening to the point I could barely breathe.

"I'm not fucking playing. I want that information, and I want it now. I know that Dale had several other offshore accounts open under that name, so you're going to tell me before I kill you," he snarled.

My eyes watered as I tried to claw at his arms, the effort useless. My body was sore, and I still felt weak from whatever drug they had given me.

Just then, the door flew open, followed by loud voices and something that sounded like a gunshot. He pressed harder on my throat until everything went black, and silence fell around me.

Thirty-Six
Patrick

I paced the entryway of the inn for what felt like hours while Gage stood by, watching me. I couldn't read the expression on his face, but I knew he was as pissed off as I was about being told to stand down. While I like Keith and valued him as a friend, right now I wanted to kick him in the nuts and tell him to go fuck himself. I wouldn't be able to rest until I knew that Poppy was alive and safe.

I glanced at my watch, noting how long it had been since he'd called and said that they'd located her. Twenty-seven minutes.

Twenty-seven minutes and no fucking follow-up on the woman I loved.

I swallowed hard, forcing myself to stay as calm as I could as my mind raced with all of the thoughts of what could have happened to her.

Just then, my phone rang.

With trembling fingers, I pulled it out and answered it.

Thirty-Seven
Poppy

I sat in the back of the ambulance while they checked my vitals again, making sure I was okay. Other than some bruising and a few scratches, everything checked out, and I was given the all-clear on the health side. The FBI was still waiting to talk to me, which wasn't surprising.

I had no idea it was them who had stormed into the cabin when I passed out, but I woke up to Patrick's friend, Keith, carrying me out of harm's way. I quickly learned that Paco was Officer Hughes' father and that he had been dating Lisa, which was how everyone was involved. In addition to the accounts Dale had opened under my name in Coyote Creek, he'd opened several others in nearby towns as well. The FBI had been monitoring all of them, including the ones I had transferred money out of earlier.

Paco, Lisa, and Officer Hughes had all been arrested and were taken to jail, while Keith stayed with me. While I had no idea about any of the stuff Dale was involved with, I was still the prime suspect in his death, and there were numerous people who wanted to question me. I knew this would be a long, drawn-out process while they attempted to gather information, but I no longer felt like I had anything to hide.

"Can you tell us about what happened the night you left?" a male FBI agent asked as Keith sat beside me. There were a few agents in the room with us, along with the Silver Falls police chief, and a few people in regular clothes, that I didn't know who they were.

"Dale had been drinking and demanded sex from me. I said no, and he attacked me," I answered, holding my hands in my lap to keep from fidgeting.

"What did you do when he attacked you?"

"I fought back the best I could."

"How so?"

"I grabbed a frying pan and hit him in the head with it several times before he fell to the ground. Once he was a safe distance away, I left," I answered, knowing that I was still telling a lie.

Some secrets would go to the grave with me, no matter what it cost me to protect them.

"Where did you go when you left?"

"I walked until I reached the highway, then I saw a semi-truck approaching and asked for a ride."

"Do you have the name of the truck driver?"

"No," I said, shaking my head. "He didn't ask for my information, and I didn't ask for his. I just wanted to get as far away from my husband as possible. He said he was heading west, so I accepted the ride to Silver Falls."

The male FBI agent looked to another agent before nodding.

"It didn't bother you to take a ride from a strange man you didn't know, given what you'd gone through with your husband?"

I knew where he was going with that, and my stomach soured. I pulled my shoulders back and sat tall as I answered him with every ounce of fire that continued to flow through me when I thought about what I had survived already.

"No. It didn't bother me because I knew that there were no options if I wanted to live. If I had stayed in Coyote Creek, Dale would have killed me. I was more than willing to take my chances with a man I didn't know and risk *everything* to get to safety because my life depended on it. I didn't have the luxury of waiting for someone else to come along and save me. I only had myself."

The agent wrote something down and then looked up at me, staring into my eyes with an intensity that felt like he was looking into my soul.

"Did you know that Sheriff Hudson had come to Silver Falls?"

"No," I answered honestly. "I had no idea he had come here until officers showed up at my boyfriend's cabin to tell me they had found Dale's body and car in the river."

"Don't you think it's a little suspicious that his body was found *here* and not in Coyote Creek, where you left him?"

"Not at all. Dale knew about Patrick and knew that he was my ex-boyfriend who lived in Silver Falls. I'm sure he figured that was where I headed when I left. It wasn't a secret that I wanted out of our marriage, as I had asked for a divorce several times. I may not have ever admitted it out loud, but I'm sure Dale knew that I was still in love with Patrick."

"If you were in love with someone else, why did you get married in Vegas?"

"I was drunk and stupid. I instantly regretted it the next day. But Dale was set on staying married, despite the fact that we weren't in love with each other. As you've already heard, there was a plan from the start with him and Paco, long before Dale and I ever got married. While it felt like a drunken, stupid mistake to me, it had been a calculated decision on Dale's end. Come to think of it, it explains why he insisted on buying so many rounds that night. He wanted to make sure I was inebriated so I couldn't say no to getting married."

The agent jotted more notes down as I shifted uncomfortably in my seat. I was exhausted and starving, just wanting to go home and get out of there. He opened his mouth to speak, but Keith held up a hand and stopped him.

"I think that's enough for today," he said, pinning the guy with a look. "She isn't leaving town, so if you'd like to interview her further, you can set up a time at the office and do it then. She's been more than accommodating as it is."

The FBI agent nodded, then stood up and walked off with the other agent, leaving me alone with Keith.

"Thank you for that," I said softly. "My head feels like it's going to explode, so I don't think I could handle much more right now."

"Totally understandable. How about I take you home so you can get some rest?"

"That sounds wonderful. Thank you."

I accepted his hand as I stood up, hating how weak I

continued to feel. While I desperately wanted to see Patrick, at this point, I just wanted to find a warm spot and sleep for a few days.

196

Thirty-Eight
Patrick

The second I heard a car door closing, I flung open the door and raced out of the inn, rushing to Poppy's side as she climbed out of the SUV. My eyes quickly scanned her face as I held my hand out to help her. She smiled softly at me, and I hated how weak she looked. *What the fuck happened to her?*

Keith climbed out and walked around the front of the SUV, giving me a nod as I held Poppy tucked into my side with my arm wrapped protectively around her. While I was thankful that he got her out safely, I was still seething that he'd made me sit on the sidelines, not knowing what was happening.

"Hey, baby," I said softly to Poppy. "Are you okay?"

She nodded and looked up at me with tears in her eyes.

"I am now."

The wind whipped around us as a gust of snow blew in our faces. I lifted my hand to shield us as I guided Poppy to the inn. Gage waited for us, holding the door open so the wind couldn't force it closed.

Once we were all inside, Gage shut the door, trapping the winter storm outside while the one raging inside of me unleashed. Poppy was already being led to the couch by her cousin when I swung around and grabbed Keith's shirt, forcing him against the wall.

His eyes didn't so much as even flash with a hint of fear as a smirk played across his lips. My jaw clenched as I stared at him, trying to find the words I wanted to say. I was torn between wanting to rip him a new asshole and thanking him for saving the woman I loved.

"Patrick, knock it off," Poppy said from the couch, the exhaustion in her voice evident.

I glanced at her over my shoulder, my heart instantly melting for this incredible woman who was still alive and safe. I let go of Keith and stepped back, shoving a hand through my hair.

"Sorry," I muttered, shaking my head.

While we were friends for as long as I could remember, I wouldn't put it past him to file charges against me for putting my hands on an FBI agent.

"Don't be. I get it. I would do the same for the woman I love," he replied, giving me a knowing smile.

Gage stiffened slightly, then let his shoulders fall as if even he couldn't be mad about Poppy and me anymore.

"Thank you," I said, feeling the knot in my throat as emotion threatened to overwhelm me. "Thank you for protecting her."

"My pleasure. But, if you don't mind, I'm gonna need to get going before I get stuck in that storm," Keith said, pointing to the window.

The snow was falling heavily in thick sheets, casting a blanket of white outside.

"I don't think you're going anywhere in that," I answered.

"I don't have much of a choice. My hotel is in town."

"You can stay here at the inn," Gage offered. "You'll be our official first guest."

"You don't have to do that," Keith insisted. "Really, I don't mind. My SUV has four-wheel drive, so I should be just fine."

"That's bullshit, and you know it. Stop being difficult and just accept you're going to be staying here for a few days," I said, watching Poppy as she yawned and leaned into the couch cushion. It would only be a matter of minutes before she was asleep.

Keith sighed heavily, letting his shoulders fall.

"Alright. I guess I don't have a choice."

"I'll show you to your room," Gage offered, leading Keith upstairs to the rooms they had been renovating.

I went and sat on the couch next to Poppy, pulling her into my arms as she quickly drifted to sleep.

Ten minutes later, Gage headed into the kitchen to work on dinner while Keith joined me in the living room. Poppy's snoring assured me she was asleep, which meant this was my time to ask Keith what the fuck had happened.

I opened my mouth to speak, but stopped when he held up his hand.

"While I am your friend, I am first and foremost an FBI

agent, which means there's a lot I cannot discuss with you," he warned.

"Okay. Well, how about we start with how the fuck you got here in the first place and why you never told me you were in Silver Falls."

He leaned back in the plush chair and rested his hands over his stomach.

"I've been here since the day after Officer Kearton was murdered," he answered.

"Why didn't you tell me?"

"I couldn't risk jeopardizing anything we were working on."

"How much did you already know?" I asked.

"We knew quite a bit and had been watching Paco Lopez for a while. After we discovered his connection to Sheriff Hudson, I took an interest in it when you told me about Poppy. I had my own team working quietly on things."

I shook my head and tried to process things as he filled me in on what he could. While Lisa had been responsible for planting the photos in my bedroom, Officer Hughes had been the one to break in. He'd also been responsible for the death of Officer Kearton. It turned out she was close to uncovering his connection to Paco Lopez, so he killed her before she could tell anyone.

It felt like the weight of the world had been lifted from my shoulders as all of the dark secrets that had been following Poppy had finally come to light. Dale had targeted her from the very beginning and used her desire to feel loved and wanted against her by creating a false sense of security that he quickly tore away. While Poppy would have more questioning to undergo regarding Dale and the illegal activities he was involved in, we could finally rest knowing that no one could hurt her anymore. The demons of his past had finally been caught.

202

Thirty-Nine
Poppy

Three days had passed since the whole ordeal with getting kidnapped and rescued and learning all of the dirty secrets of my dead husband. It had been nice staying at the inn, especially since Gage didn't give us a hard time about Patrick sleeping in my room, which meant he must've accepted that there was nothing that would keep us apart at this point.

Once the storm had passed and the roads were safe, Keith left, promising to keep us updated on when he got home. He'd filled us in on the woman he had waiting for him in Colorado and how he was planning to propose to her on Christmas. With it only being two days away, we wished him well and asked for pictures as soon as she said yes.

I sat on the couch, holding my coffee mug to my chest as a blanket covered my lap while Gage and Patrick talked outside. It felt weird not having to worry about looking over our shoulders or having a constant threat looming in the distance. While I had seen them arrest Paco, Lisa, and Officer Hughes, it still felt surreal to me that everything was over.

The front door opened, and Patrick headed inside while Gage stayed outside, clearing the driveway.

"What's going on?" I asked, nodding to my cousin through the window.

"Julie and Daisy are on their way home, so he's clearing the driveway for them," Patrick answered as he sat beside me on the couch.

"He does realize that it's still snowing, right?"

"Yeah, but to him, that doesn't matter. He wants to make it as safe as possible for his girls when they get home."

"I love how much he loves them," I said softly, smiling warmly as I turned and looked at Patrick. "Almost as much as I love you."

"No one could ever love anyone as much as *I* love *you*," he countered, brushing his lips lightly against mine.

"Since he's clearing the driveway, does that mean we can head out and go back to the cabin?" I asked, my voice too hopeful, giving me away.

"Baby, even if the driveway wasn't clear, I would hoist you over my shoulder and carry you the two miles to my cabin if that's what you wanted."

"Well, I am *pretty sure* he heard us last night, and I can't guarantee that I'll be able to stay quiet for much longer… so… yeah…"

Patrick stood up, grabbed my coffee cup from my hands, and set it on the coffee table before reaching down and putting me over his shoulder.

"Patrick!" I squealed, laughter erupting from me. "What are you doing?"

"Taking you home where you belong. Though I hate to tell you that I don't think two miles is going to do anything to keep them from hearing you tonight."

He tossed the blanket onto the couch and started walking to the door.

"I don't have any of my stuff," I said, still laughing.

"We'll get it later."

"I don't even have shoes! Or my phone."

He stopped and looked over his shoulder as I looked up at him.

"I'll buy you new everything, Poppy. I don't give a fuck about any of that right now. All I want is to take you home and devour you like the delicious treat you are. We can worry about the rest later."

He slapped my ass, sending a jolt of excitement through me, before he opened the door and walked past Gage.

"Thanks for everything," he said, walking far enough past that I caught the grin on my cousin's face as he continued to clear the driveway. "We'll see you on Christmas. Don't call or text or come over until then."

"Noted," Gage replied, shaking his head as I let mine fall, getting the perfect view of Patrick's tight ass in the gray sweatpants he had on.

Typically, I would have hated it if a man had carried me like this, but it turned out I loved everything Patrick did. He had a way of making me feel safe and protected at all times, even when he did depraved things to my body. We hadn't been fully alone in what felt like months, which meant we were going to spend the next two days getting our fill of each other without having to worry about anyone else being there.

<u>Forty</u>
Patrick

I watched Poppy with such intensity that I didn't miss the look in her eyes as she pulled her hair up with the Christmas-themed hair tie she'd picked up at Silver Falls Express when she first got here. I loved that she had a thing for silly, Christmas-themed things like the candy cane pen and the Christmas straw toppers—but seeing her tie her hair up on top of her head before stalking over to suck my cock was a new level of appreciation for the Christmas spirit. Not only that, she was wearing a lacy red bra and matching panties that had me feeling all sorts of jolly.

"Have you been a good boy?" she purred, looking up at me from under her thick lashes, batting them as she rubbed her hand up my thigh before sliding it over my boxer briefs, feeling my erection.

"Good. Bad. I'll be whatever you want me to be, baby."

We'd already spent the past day and a half fucking nonstop, but it seemed we couldn't get enough of each other. It was Christmas Eve, and we were supposed to go to my parents' condo for dinner tonight. At the rate we were going, I was going to have to cancel and make it up to everyone on New Year's Day.

"Only good boys get rewarded," she said, licking her lips as she lowered the waistband of my boxer briefs and pulled my cock out. "And I *really* want to reward you."

"I've been good." I closed my eyes and hissed as her tongue slid across the tip of my cock, making it harden in her hand. "Oh, so fucking good."

She hummed her approval as she opened her mouth and slid me inside. I gripped the sheets beneath me as I sat on the edge of the bed, desperate to keep my sanity after she'd spent the whole morning making me come undone. By two o'clock this morning, I'd lost count of how many orgasms Poppy had after we reached the double digits. To say we had a fucking problem would be an understatement.

I looked down and found her eyes on me as she opened her mouth further, taking my cock all the way to the back of her throat while stroking my shaft with her hand. It felt so incredible, but as much as I loved getting head from her, I loved fucking her tight pussy more.

"Baby, you gotta stop, or I'm going to come," I warned, out of breath and desperate to fuck her. "I want to come in your pussy, not your mouth."

She whimpered and sucked harder, increasing her speed while she gave me a taunting look. Poppy had learned quickly that even though I came, I could stay hard and come again within ten to fifteen minutes.

I gently reached down and dug my fingers into her hair, not caring that I was messing up the messy bun she'd just put in. I closed my eyes and held on as Poppy brought me to another mind-blowing orgasm as ropes of cum shot down the back of her throat.

When I was done, she slowly pulled away and wiped the corners of her mouth as she stared at me like the little minx she was.

I took a deep breath and slowly let it out as I studied her, loving the way she squirmed beneath my gaze.

"I thought I said I wanted to come in your pussy, not your mouth," I said, arching an eyebrow.

She shrugged and chewed her nail nervously as she watched me with a huge grin on her face.

"I did what I wanted to do. Consider it a *Christmas gift*, if you will."

"Christmas isn't until tomorrow, and you not listening seems to have put you on the naughty list."

"Oh no. Whatever will I do?" she deadpanned, pretending to be upset about it as she threw as much sarcasm as she could into her voice.

I leaned forward and rested my elbows on my knees as I looked at her and sighed. She sat submissively with her hands in her lap as she waited for me to tell her what her punishment was.

"Stand up," I demanded, pinning her with a look that sent a flush of red over her cheeks.

She did as I asked and stood in front of me. I slid my hand up her thigh, noticing the goosebumps that spread across her skin as I moved higher, pushing her panties to the side as I felt the warm wetness between her legs.

"Look at how wet you are, just begging for this cock," I murmured as I leaned in and kissed her stomach softly. "But only good girls get cock, Poppy."

She moaned and slid her fingers into my hair, pulling it slightly as I removed my hand.

I stood up, forcing her to take a few steps back, and walked behind her. She stood still, waiting as my fingers skimmed over the skin on her back before unclasping her bra. I pulled the straps down her arms and then tossed it to the floor, leaving her in just the panties.

"Your body is perfection," I whispered in her ear as I stood behind her while my hands caressed her heavy breasts, my cock twitching at the thought of sucking her nipples. "The things I'm going to do to it…"

Another soft moan escaped her lips as she rested her head against my chest, allowing my hands to explore her body. But I wanted so much more than that.

"Get on the bed, facing the wall on your hands and knees," I said, pulling away and breaking the trance she was under.

She smiled over her shoulder before doing as I asked.

I opened the nightstand drawer and pulled out the candy cane-shaped vibrator I had purchased online from Dark Vibes. It was supposed to be a Christmas gift, but I wasn't about to wait. I wanted to bring her all of the pleasure I could now and watch her fall apart like she did with the last toy we had used.

I pushed the button, grinning when the silence of the room was broken with the gentle buzzing sound of the toy. Poppy's head whipped around, her eyes wide as she stared at it.

"Turn around and be a good girl, or I'm not going to show you what it can do," I warned, taking my time before I got on the bed behind her. I wanted to build the anticipation, but I was already hard and ready to come again.

I pulled Poppy's panties to the side and slowly guided my cock to her entrance. We'd already decided against using protection after having a conversation about it early on. While she was on birth control, there was something intoxicating about the thought of getting her pregnant and having her carry my child. It was something we both wanted and hadn't put a timeframe on when we would officially start trying.

She hissed as I pushed deeper inside of her, my hand gripping her hip as I relished in how good her pussy felt wrapped around my cock.

"Fuck, Patrick," she moaned, arching her back slightly. "Why do you always feel so good?"

"Because this pussy is mine, Poppy. It's my job to make it feel good and make sure that you're always satisfied."

"I would be more satisfied if you fuc—"

Her words were cut off with a slight yelp as I turned the candy cane vibrator on and pressed it directly against her clit.

"FUCK! FUCK! FUCK!" she screamed, squirming as she tried to get away from the overwhelming sensation.

But I was a man on a mission, and making my girlfriend come so hard they could hear her two towns over was my only goal. I pulled out and slammed back inside of her, making sure to keep the toy on her clit. I knew she loved it rough and deep, and I was going to give her exactly what she needed.

I kept my balance as I continued to thrust hard and deep, increasing my pace as I felt her tighten around me. Within seconds, she let out a loud, throaty moan as she came hard on my cock, forcing me to release my load inside of her.

Turned out it was going to be a white Christmas after all.

Forty-One
Poppy

I shifted on the couch, trying to get comfortable, but my body was sore from all of the pleasure Patrick had given me over the past few days. Julie gave me a strange look for a split second until her mouth turned into a huge smile as she realized what was happening.

A blush covered my cheeks as I looked away and tried to focus on Daisy as she opened our gift. I loved that Patrick had taken so much time picking the perfect gifts for her, but I couldn't help the way my heart felt when she opened the scarf that I knitted for her. I'd noticed she hadn't been wearing one, and when I asked Julie about it, she said Daisy had lost the one she had and that they needed to buy her a new one. I found out what her favorite colors were and bought some yarn when Patrick took me to Silver Falls Express before everything happened.

It was still weird not worrying about someone wanting to hurt me, and I had a hard time accepting that not only was I finally safe, but I was also finally somewhere where I felt wanted and loved. It had been a long time since I'd felt that way with family, but being around Gage and Julie made me realize just how much I had been missing. While I had no desire to have a relationship with my parents, I couldn't see myself *not* being around my new family.

Daisy continued opening her presents as everyone watched. We'd gone to dinner at Patrick's parents' house last night for Christmas Eve, and it had been such a wonderful night. They welcomed me into their family so easily that I found myself constantly waiting for the other shoe to drop. I knew that my past would always be a part of me and that I had learned from the mistakes I'd made along the way, but it was surreal not having anyone hold those over my head. I'd grown up constantly expecting the worst, so it was hard to get used to people only wanting the best for me, but I was learning to let them love me.

Once everyone finished opening their gifts, the adults headed into the kitchen to work on dinner while Patrick pulled me to the side. We stood in front of the Christmas tree that lit up the entryway of the inn. I looked around, wondering what was wrong, when suddenly he dropped to his knee and looked up at me as he pulled a small black box out of his pocket. He carefully opened it, revealing a gorgeous diamond ring with a rose-gold band.

I swallowed hard and covered my mouth with my hands as the room got quiet. I glanced up to find his parents, Gage, and Julie all watching from the living room while Daisy played with Travis and Duke.

"My life hasn't been the same since the day I saw you standing in the middle of the forest, trying to do something you never should have had to do. I never knew what it was like to love someone so deeply that I would literally burn the world down to keep them safe until I met you. Poppy, you've changed my life in so many ways, and I can't imagine spending another day without you. Will you please do me the honor of marrying me and being my wife so I can spend the rest of my life loving you the way you deserve to be loved?"

I nodded and didn't bother stopping the tears that slid down my cheeks as he grinned and took the ring out of the box before sliding it on my finger. He stood up, and I wrapped my arms around his neck as he wrapped his around my waist. We held each other tightly as I continued to cry, this time from pure happiness.

"I love you so much," I said softly. "I cannot wait to marry you."

"I love you more, and I promise, I'm going to spend the rest of my days making sure you know just how much that is."

I pulled back and looked at his beautiful face, refusing to let go of him just yet.

"I'm going to do the same. I'm going to love you so hard you'll get tired of me," I teased, knowing the second he caught my secret innuendo with the way his eyes darkened.

"No fucking chance that will ever happen," he growled as he leaned in and nipped my ear. "Give me two minutes, and I'll come up with an excuse for us to leave so I can take you home and show you just how hard you can love me."

I giggled and smacked his shoulder, stepping away as our family approached.

Gage pulled me in for a hug first, holding me tightly as he congratulated me.

"I'm so happy for you," he said, his eyes showing he meant it. "I love that you're going to stick around and keep this one on his toes. He's needed someone to get him in line for a while now."

"Happy to do it,' I teased, stepping back as he let go of me. Julie swooped in next, wrapping me in a warm embrace while Gage and Patrick had their moment.

"Does that mean I get to be a flower girl twice?" Daisy asked, joining us as she looked at her mom, then at me.

I quickly turned and looked at Julie, catching a guilty smile on her face. She lifted her hand and wiggled her fingers, the engagement ring catching in the light.

"Oh my God!" I squealed, gently pulling her hand over so I could see the beautiful ring. "Julie! I'm so happy for you guys! Why didn't you say anything?"

"We were planning to tell everyone during dinner," Julie replied with a shrug. She looked past me to my cousin, and I noticed a look that passed between them, almost as if there was more they weren't telling us. "Gage proposed last night."

"Fucker," Patrick muttered playfully. "Always have to be first."

"Hey, when I see something I want, I go for it." Gage shrugged.

"Well, congratulations to you guys, too!" I exclaimed, putting an end to the chess match that was about to start between them. "Looks like we'll have lots of fun wedding planning to do together. Who knows, maybe we can all get married here at the inn."

"Great minds think alike," Julie said, giving me another genuine smile.

After everyone finished hugging and congratulating each other, Patrick and I lingered behind while the others returned to the kitchen to get started on dinner.

Patrick opened his arms, pulling me into his chest as I accepted his embrace.

"They might have beat us by getting engaged first, but I say we show them a thing or two and I go home and knock you up," he said playfully, wiggling his eyebrows.

"I don't know, I think they might have more secrets they haven't shared yet," I responded, catching Julie's eye from across the room. She blushed and looked away, pretending to be focused on cutting an onion as Gage hugged her from behind.

"Maybe I can force him to spill the beans at dinner," Patrick said, glancing over his shoulder to look at them.

"Na, let it go. Some secrets deserve to be kept." I leaned up and pressed a kiss to his lips, loving that he knew what I meant.

****

Want more holiday romance? Be sure to check out my Sugarplum Falls series! You can grab Blame It On The Mistletoe for free! https://books2read.com/u/bw1rqe

Come hang out and chat about books with us in my reader group, Samantha Baca's Smutties! I'd love to hang out with you! https://www.facebook.com/groups/2945710968775398/

218

Other Books By Samantha Baca

<u>Romantic Suspense</u>

The Haven Brook Series (small town romantic suspense):

'Til Death Do Us Part (Haven Brook Book 1) | The Cradle Will Fall (Haven Brook Book 2) | The Ties That Bind (Haven Brook Book 3) | A Very Haven Christmas (Haven Brook Book 4- Novella) | Three Strikes, You're Gone (Haven Brook Book 5)

The Dark Shadows Trilogy (romantic suspense)

Five Steps Ahead (Dark Shadows Book 1) |Ten Seconds Too Late (Dark Shadows Book 2) | Against The Clock (Dark Shadows Book 3)

Broken (Standalone)

Silver Falls Duet (small town holiday romantic suspense):

Snowed Inn For Christmas | Murder and Mistletoe

<u>Romantic Comedy</u>

Beaumont Creek Series (small town)

Just One Time | Second Chances | Third Time's The Charm | Four-ever Single | Fifth Wheel

Whiskey Mountain Series

Something To Talk About | Something To Think About | Something To Believe In | Something To Live For

<u>Holiday</u>

Sugarplum Falls Series (Holiday Novellas- can be read as standalone)

Blame It On The Mistletoe | Blame It On The Eggnog | Blame It On The Candy Canes
Blame It On The Blizzard | Blame It On The Reindeer | Blame It On The Carols | Blame It On The Lattes | Blame It On The Secret Santa | Blame It On The Holidays: A collection of bonus epilogues

The Stone Creek Series (small town novellas)

Chocolate Covered Mistletoe (Stone Creek Book 1) | Candy Coated Promises (Stone Creek Book 2) | Pumpkin Spiced Possibilities (Stone Creek Book 3)

Silver Falls Duet (Small town romantic suspense novellas)

Snowed Inn For Christmas | Murder and Mistletoe

Standalone Holiday Novellas

Snow Place To Go | A Very Merry Kissmas | A Christmas Wish | Holiday Hijinks

Standalone Holiday Full Length

Wild Winter

<u>Standalone Books</u>

One Last Wish | Finding Love In Apartment 2C (novella) | Breaking All The Rules (Previously published as: Cocky Counsel: A Hero Club Novel | All Is Fair In Food And War (novella)

Acknowledgments

As always, I would like to thank the readers for taking the time to read my book and escape into a fun adventure! This book was so much fun to write, and I truly hope you've enjoyed the Silver Falls Duet! I loved mixing two genres I love writing in to create this steamy, holiday romantic suspense set in a small town!

Thank you to my alpha and beta readers for taking the time to help me with this one. Valerie, Malissa, Claire, Azucena, Karrie, Reina, and Jennifer, I appreciate all the feedback you ladies provided! A huge shout-out to Kaylyn as well for doing a final read-through on this one for me!

To my family and close friends who always support me and shout my name out anytime someone mentions they like steamy romance—thank you. I appreciate the constant love and friendship! It means the world to me!

I've done acknowledgments over forty times now, but I still like to give a huge shout-out to my incredibly supportive husband for everything he does to make this dream of mine possible. From listening to me ramble about story ideas for hours to helping me format my books, he goes above and beyond, and I will forever be grateful. Thank you, my love, for everything you do!

And last, but not least, I want to say how much I love my sweet girls, and that even though they've gotten older, they haven't stopped being my biggest fans. Thank you for loving me and my spicy books so much that you tell your teachers and everyone you meet that your mom writes steamy romance! I love you both so much!

About the Author

Samantha lives in the southwest with her husband and two children, where she enjoys writing, drinking iced coffee, and watching the greatest show of all time—Friends. With over 30 books published, Samantha enjoys writing across several different genres, from steamy romantic suspense to laugh-out-loud spicy romantic comedies. She also has a sweet spot for holiday stories, so grab a blanket and get ready to binge some of the sweetest—yet spicy—holiday romance your heart can handle!

Samantha loves connecting with her readers, so here's a list of where you can find her:

Facebook Reader Group:

https://www.facebook.com/groups/2945710968775398/

Facebook:

https://www.facebook.com/AuthorSamanthaBaca

Instagram:

https://instagram.com/author_samantha_baca

Webpage:

www.samanthabaca.com

Goodreads:

http://www.goodreads.com/authorsamanthabaca

Books2Read:

https://books2read.com/ap/RQAYK9/Samantha-Baca